More Than Friends

Michela Rubin

Contents

Chapter 1

I just couldn't keep my eyes open at that moment. I was driving myself home after a hectic day at the office. An usual day in my busy life.

Being a game developer was taking a toll on my sleeping habits.

I remembered my mom's voice through the phone nagging me to go to sleep early but I stayed awake all night busy catching Pokémon.

You can ask me why would any sane person do that. I was just staying awake to analyze the competetor's work. I was doing my job. Sure, let me live in delusion for some more time.

And look at where it got me now. I felt like I was on a different planet and I could see the Pokémon dancing in front of me. On the road. Only I couldn't seem to catch them.

Normally I was not the one to drive irresponsibly during such tough times. Yes, I know.

But my so-called bestie Rose ditched me for going on a date with her new boyfriend. I didn't have any other options. It was late and I couldn't get any Uber.

No points for guessing that I don't have other friends as I confessed about my nightly routine of escaping to the virtual world. You might think that my weekend routine would look different. Well, think again.

What about someone other than a friend? You might wonder. I have been on dates but I haven't had a serious boyfriend in my whole life. I concentrated on my studies till college so that I wouldn't lose my scholarship.

Do you expect me to suddenly become some kind of relationship expert when I came out of college? Old habits die hard. No, I am not talking about the movie. It was an awesome movie though. See, this is how my mind works.

I wasn't interested in going to parties to find someone drunk enough to listen to my work talk. And then it would not be the same on the next day when sobriety hits.

Rose was forcing me to go on blind dates but I was not the one to make good first impressions. Don't think I am exaggerating. You will see that in action soon.

It doesn't mean I had low self esteem. I wasn't exactly un-likeable. I just wanted to acknowledge that I was not an easy person to date.

You might need more details than this if you were to fill the hospital form for me in the future. Or God forbid, post my bail. Wait, I am getting ahead of myself.

I am Alex and I am working as a developer in a gaming start-up called Dez. I am definitely not a drama queen as you suspect. I am a normal guy with a little bit of sleep deprivation problem.

That might exactly sound like something a crazy person pretending to be normal would say. If I were you, I would be skeptical too. But stay with me.

Logical part of my brain was asking me to stop the car but that part was effectively silenced by the sleep demon inside me.

I could almost hear my mom saying, "Alex, I told you it's all because of that stupid job. Take a vacation and come stay with us for a while".

When I was arguing with my mom in my imagination, a car sped past me to the front and then slowed down a bit. I noticed it a bit late and hit the brakes just on time.

I finally came back to my senses and realized I almost hit another car as I wasn't paying attention.

I parked safely on the side of the road and got down to check if I have caused any damage and came face to face with the most handsome guy I have ever seen in my life.

He had blue eyes. I think. Or was it green? Well, he had eyes. Pretty eyes.

Ok, seriously? I needed to get some quality sleep. Who would describe a guy's eyes they just met as pretty? Probably me, in my heightened state of sleep deprivation.

I could see his face thanks to the car light and he had all the features you could read in a book about a hot bad guy. Maybe not bad but definitely hot. Brown hair. Tall. Muscular. Attractive. You get the gist.

I couldn't believe myself. Why was I wondering about the color of his eyes when I almost caused an accident?

I needed to apologize and I should probably pay for any damages. God. I hoped I didn't make a dent on his shiny car. It looked expensive.

He looked somewhat calm too. My immediate thought was "Wow! Nothing happened. I can't believe my luck today". I never thought I would mean it sarcastically until he opened his mouth.

Chapter 2

"Are you sleep-driving? Is that a thing? Do you want me to take you to a hospital?"

I was going to remember the first thing he said to me, for a long long time. I didn't realize my mouth was open until his words made me snap back to reality. I subtly tried to hide the fact that I was indeed staring at him.

My brilliant reply was "Yes. I mean, no, I am fine. Sorry, I wasn't paying attention for a bit. It's totally my fault. Did I say I was sorry?". Yeah, thanks brain. I didn't expect you to take revenge on me like this. Not in front of a good looking guy.

He smirked and said, "Yes, just a few hundred times. Are you in a condition to drive?"

I was wondering if he would drive me if I said no. Wait, what? I wasn't thinking about getting in a car with a stranger, Was I? Haven't I learned anything from binge-watching criminal files and Law & Order? Get a grip, Alex.

"Yes, I can, thank you very much. I will make it back if no one tries to cut me off. Like someone here did." I replied coldly even though it was my fault. Something about his smirk irritated me.

I winced at my own words and got ready to receive an earful as that would be the common response by any sane person at that moment. But instead he decided to give me a heart attack. "You are such a baby, Aren't you?"

"No, you are the baby". I silently cursed myself for being sleep deprived. That was the only reason I couldn't think of good come-backs. Yes, I am sure. If I was at my best, I would have said "Babies don't need to drive themselves. Haha". Not good enough? Ok, you got me.

But I couldn't form coherent sentences at that moment. I mean, did you get a good look at him? I should thank my lucky stars I didn't faint when he looked at me with that stupid smile.

He was getting on my nerves a little and at the same time I couldn't stop staring at him. Lethal combination, if you ask me. I could not figure if I wanted to punch him or ask for his number. Wait, what? I needed to leave before I did something crazy.

He looked at his watch and sighed. "You can call me baby. Or Dean. I don't mind. Go and sleep it off. Try not to kill anyone on your way."

I was way too tired to argue and nodded. Even his name was sexy. Stop it, Alex. It wasn't like me to go all fanboy on a guy I just met. Or anyone for that matter.

Also, it was not like I was going to see him again. Why should I waste my precious time on some hot stranger? Ugh, I mean with some weird stranger.

I needed to go back before I say anything embarrassing. I could safely say I crossed that limit on my mind for one day. "Thanks! You too. I am really sorry. Bye, Dean".

He looked at me like he was having a debate inside his head and finally said, "Bye, Alex. Drive safely".

With that he walked back to his car and drove away.

I started my car and drove back home as carefully as possible. Because I was responsible. Not because he told me to.

I had dinner and called my mom before going to sleep. I decided against playing games even when my mobile tried to lure me with thousands of notifications. I have learned my lesson.

"Dear brain, I'm going to spoil you with 8 hours of quality sleep. You better be ready with good comebacks next time I meet a hand-so- I mean arrogant guy. With love, Alex."

I shook my head at my own thoughts and closed my eyes. My brain decided to show me a highlight reel of my evening without leaving out any of the embarrassing details.

Do you think I should have asked his number? How do people start dating? If I met him at a different situation, would I have hit on him? If we met somewhere else I doubted if he would have even talked to me. That seemed impossible. He might have had a lot of choices. Oh my God, why would I assume that he was single in the first place?

This world was not a kind enough place to leave hot guys like him to be single for long. Or even worse, what if he was a player?

Yeah, Alex, so what if he was? Why would you care in the first place? I didn't have any answer to my own questions. "Fine, you win", I surrendered. You see? Totally normal to have a conversation with myself.

Who was I kidding? I was attracted to him. I couldn't get his face out of my mind. Don't even get started on his voice. I loved the way he said my name.

Suddenly the thought hit me like a wave. I never told him my name. But how the heck did he know that?

Did I say something else too without realizing it? God, I hope not.

Chapter 3

When I woke up the next day, I was almost sure it was all a dream. If that was the case, good job, brain! But even I was not that creative.

Was it my brain's way of begging me to get a good night's sleep once in a while? Nah, it felt way too real. I could still picture his smirk and I remember the way I kept reacting to each of his words. Sadly, I remembered every embarrassing comeback that escaped my mouth.

Maybe my brain got super advanced from all the games I have been playing. I mean, it could happen, right? Creating a simulation for a dating game? Ugh, I need to get some coffee.

I vowed to listen to myself and to never drive when I'm sleepy after yesterday's incident. What if I actually fell asleep? What if I didn't hit the brakes on time?

Those thoughts were disturbing me and my brain suddenly decided it was the best moment to throw in the image of the mysterious guy I met who knew my name.

Ugh. I felt like the narrator of a thriller novel. A cringe-worthy one at that. Let me know how is "My hot stalker" an option for the title. Never mind, it sounds dirty.

I decided it was time to stop after I got stuck in a loop of thinking about his pretty eyes and how bizarre the whole encounter was. I must have told my name and forgot about it when he smiled at me. That's completely plausible given the state I was in yesterday. I mean sleep-deprived. Not frustrated. Not at all.

Was thinking about it worth leaving my coffee to get cold? Nothing is worth it.

There is only one way to get some peace of mind. That was asking him directly if I ever see him again. Sigh. The thought excited and worried me at the same time.

Did I want to see him again? No. But yes. Imagine seeing his smile again. No, Alex. But I just wanted to ask that question.

What was I trying to convince myself for? Let's say for the sake of argument, I meet him again and ask how did he know my name. He might think I was weird, if he didn't already assumed. Or he might introduce his date and I might end up with a broken heart.

If I were to ignore this and move on, it would just be a memory, somewhat weird but a good one. Heck, it might even provide me with some well deserved laughter when I think about it in the future. I chose the blissful ignorance.

I started to get ready for what I hoped and prayed - an uneventful and forgettable day. I was happy with the solution my delusional brain came up with and who was I to even question it?

I picked up my friend Rose from her home at 9. She was really enthusiastic to see me.

I later realized how naive I was to even think that. She was looking forward not to see me but to brag about her date.

"Have I mentioned it? Jake is a really nice guy. He could be my soulmate." Yeah, I heard it the first time and when she said it for the fifteenth time. I lost my count after twenty.

Well, I wish I could say that I tuned her out then. But no. Never. She made sure I heard every sentence by repeating it till I got annoyed.

Once she finished her rendition of the 'oh-so-perfect' date with Jake, I thought of sharing my bizarre story but I decided against it.

She would definitely think I was not taking care of myself and putting myself in danger. She was too worrying for her own good.

Rose and I have been close friends for almost 10 years now. She was a nice girl. Many of our friends have asked if we were together.

But we never thought of each other in that way. She was like a sister that I never wanted but I loved her like one.

On any other day she would have studied my face and questioned me until I gave up the information.

But today she was high on the memories of her date. She probably thought I was just not sleeping enough as usual.

When we arrived at work, she looked at me with concern and said, "Leave early and get some rest today, Alex. You look like a zombie."

I nodded and walked to my cabin. Who doesn't like to work when that 'job' involves playing games? Shh. We called it 'research'.

Anyway, I would not have much free time once I started my next sprint in a week. That would be good for my heart though. Being busy might make me forget about weird strangers.

However, blue-green eyes were haunting me during my dedicated game time. I mean 'research' time.

I had to get an extra cup or two of my caffeine fix to get through the day. Not that I was complaining.

Finally the evening came and I finally got what I prayed for. A brand new car waiting for me in the parking lot. Just kidding. I wished for an uneventful and forgettable day, remember? But why was I disappointed to get what I wanted?

I got home early and decided to get some rest. I must have been really tired after all the 'research'. I fell asleep as soon as my head hit the pillow.

Chapter 4

I didn't think I would see him again soon. Ok I was lying. I might or might not have been looking for a familiar pair of blue-green eyes in local cafes and bookstores.

What? Those are the places I frequent. But it might not be his scene. He looked like someone who liked going to loud places and mingle with people. I could just imagine him being the life of any party.

I scolded myself for stereotyping based on his looks. But the books I have read and shows I have watched taught me exactly the same thing.

Even if I met him, what would I say? Or even worse, why would he remember me? But again, he might remember me as the "weird sleepy guy who almost put a dent in his car". Heck, who wouldn't want to be remembered as 'the one who acted like a baby'?

But you know me, I have prepared a mental monolog to recite to him if I ever come face to face with him again. Well, wouldn't I like that?

So that's why I was shocked to finally see the familiar pair of eyes that were haunting me for some days. And not just in dreams.

All my preparations went out of the window when I saw him. Monolog, who? My brain felt as if I did a factory reset recently and very empty. He had that power over me even if we just met once. Human mind works in mysterious ways, huh?

So I tried to look nonchalant as much I could possibly pull-off. But, hey, if I could act that well, I would be in a movie with Sandra Bullocks or Meryl Streep and not here looking like I just swallowed a piece of gum.

Anyway, this was not the place I had in mind for our most awaited reunion. If it was not already clear, I was the one who was doing all the waiting.

It might not be even in your top 10 guesses. Ok, no more suspense. It was in front of a gas station restroom. What were the chances?

Wait, before you think I went crazy and looked for him there, let me correct you. I was not that desperate and it was not what happened.

It was a beautiful evening. Beautiful because I was going home early for some well deserved rest after a hectic day of work and meetings. No more 'research' as the next sprint started.

I was on my way to enjoy any introvert's dream destination, their own room. But I had to stop at a gas station to get some fuel for my car and take care of some urgent business.

Life lesson #436 - Don't drink a tall glass of orange juice before starting your car.

So much for taking care of my health by cutting caffeine. I knew there would be side effects if I gave up coffee.

When I came out of the restroom I saw him and immediately froze on my tracks. He didn't seem to share my reaction though.

How could he always stay calm and look cool? Look at me, probably gaping like a fish.

I tried to look uninterested and failed. Remember my confession about my non-existent proficiency in acting?

My brain was asking me to confirm if his eyes were blue or green. Not now, brain.

I could figure it out today if I just stare at him for a couple more seconds. He wouldn't mind, right? It seemed like he did. He cleared his throat awkwardly.

I snapped out of it and I had to say something to cover my tracks. Immediately. "Hello! You're David, right? What are you doing here?"

Wow. Thanks brain. I sacrificed my game time and spoiled you with all the sleep and this is what I get in return?

He raised an eyebrow and said, "It's Dean, baby. And why do people come to restroom? To pee, of course."

I was shocked at his response and all I could say was, "I am not baby. I'm Alex and you know it".

He still looked amused. "Yeah, I know".

I decided to be brave and confront him. Serial killers and bad guys wouldn't look like this, would they? But yes, this might have been some poor guy's thought too before getting stuffed in the back of an unmarked van. Ok, no more true crime podcasts for a week.

"How do you know my name?" I asked him. It was now or never.

He was confused for a second. "You told me on that day. Remember? You almost hit me and I saved you like a hero".

My brain said he side-tracked me from my question successfully but my mouth seemed to have a mind on its own. I should start listening to my brain more. But most of the time it is of no help so I tune it out.

"Like a hero? I don't remember seeing you in a suit". Wouldn't it be a sight for my sore eyes?

"What if I forgot it at the laundromat? What if I were the Superman?"

I shook my head at his antics to provoke me. "Oh, yeah? Nice to meet you, then. I'm Batman. Same laundromat". I whispered for some dramatic effect.

He laughed out loud and I felt something when I heard the sound of his laughter. I shook myself from that thought and prepared to leave. It was fun and he was easy to talk to. But it would not be easy to get the feelings involved.

Staying here wouldn't do any good for my heart. I think we have already established that. Let me save my last shred of dignity by escaping out of here. It wasn't too late for that, right?

"Oh, look at the time. I have a date with my bed. Bye Dean. See ya". With that I turned to leave. I prayed that I sounded casual and not like a sad puppy leaving it's home.

What he did next was not something I was prepared for. He stopped me by pulling back the collar of my shirt and asked "When?"

Chapter 5

I felt him pulling back my collar slightly to stop me. I was startled but in a pleasant way. Does that make any sense to you? Because it was all new for me.

He asked me "When?". I never knew I wouldn't be able to answer a simple one word question. It was tougher than all of my hardest exams combined.

"Well. I don't know. Soon. I mean later. Maybe". I sighed. Why can't I come up with fully formed sentences when I am with this guy? I could no longer blame my poor sleep schedule. There must be something wrong with my brain. They say healing starts with acceptance. Let's heal.

But wait, he was waiting for an answer. Was I supposed to reply him? When could I see him again? No, it was more like why did he want to see me again?

Ok dear brain, here's an idea. Come up with something, we could always cancel it later. Anything. I was not asking my brain for a frigging monolog. Just a decent sentence.

I stood there looking confused without any help from my poor brain. Shocking, right? He must have pitied me and thought of answering my unasked question "Why?"

He just smiled and said, "We have become too close to meet just by coincidences. Don't you think?"

"Too close? I couldn't even remember your name".

I should check my pants for any burn marks. You know how the insightful saying "liar liar" goes, right? I was not so sure if "fire in the pants" part was just there for the rhyme.

He was unaffected by my sarcastic remark. It was like he expected it.

"It's Dean, baby. I am sure you might have even had a few dreams about me and called my name". He had the nerve to add a wink.

I felt myself blushing a little on that note. I wanted to tell I didn't dream about him. But I couldn't trust my mushy brain to conjure up a witty comeback now.

It seemed to have a melt down whenever I thought of him. How could I expect it to work when the mysterious blue-green eyes winked at me.

I wanted to give up. "Fine. What do you want now? Tell me so that I can go home and sleep".

Nowadays I enjoy sleeping more. Not that I was expecting to dream about him or anything. You know. Sleeping is nice. You should try it.

"Can I get your number? I don't have my phone with me now. Can you write it on my hand? Here". He seemed little nervous.

I was speechless. Who comes out without a mobile phone these days? Anyway I was enjoying the fact that he could get nervous too.

He was teasing me a few minutes ago. He could be taken down a peg or two.

Why should I be the only one who resembled all types of emoticons you typically see on the mobile?

I held his hand lightly and wrote my number across his palm. The simple touch gave me a million butterflies. May be not a million. A decent number.

I prayed that I didn't show it on my face. Was it even considered as hand-holding? I needed to ask Rose.

"There. Now shall I leave?" I needed to leave before he finds out about the butterflies that came out of nowhere. I mean where were the flowers? How would they live without flowers?

Dear brain, stop ranting for a second. If only you spent this much effort to come up with sentences which can be said out loud and not land me in an asylum.

He was looking at his hand and he looked ecstatic. Yes, ecstatic. I was not the one to use the word carelessly but I couldn't find a way to describe the look on his face.

"I will give you a call later. We can meet for some coffee. I am new around here so I don't know about the cool hangout spots".

I laughed at his enthusiastic comment and teased, "Oh! I will be your guide, then. Always at your service, sir".

His smile was unaffected and he waved at me as I was leaving.

"No, I have Siri for that. I just wanted to see you again. Bye, baby. I mean, Alex". He corrected when he saw me scowling at him.

With that I came back home and played games for sometime. I kept losing because I was so busy being distracted by my own thoughts.

Wait, did he say he wanted to see me again? Should I have been sucked it up and asked if he was single? So what if he said no? I could start the process of moving on, which wasn't supposed to be easy.

But how could you casually ask if someone was single without making yourself so obvious? Even if he said yes, should I have asked him out? At least I would know his answer and not trying to guess it and losing sleep now.

I called my mom for our daily catch-up. I heard all about uncle Patrick and his beekeeping hobby. Ask me how he found out his new love interest was allergic to bees. It was hilarious.

Grateful for the distraction, I tried to sleep early as I didn't want my dream time to be cut short just because I actually saw him today.

Chapter 6

I would be lying if I said I wasn't expecting a call. Can't he at least text? The standard protocol dictates to call or text within few hours after you got the number, right?

Why was I disappointed? He might have lost my number. Yes, that could happen. The ink might have smudged.

Did I write it with a waterproof pen? I was not a psycho to carry waterproof pen with me. If I knew he would ask, I might have brought one.

He could have washed his hands for dinner. How could he do that when he was the one asked for my number? Was he just playing with me? No, his expressions were genuine.

I was getting tired of making a conversation with myself. I was not that helpful. You are used to it by now, right?

I was chanting "Don't think about him" repeatedly which kind of defeated its whole purpose.

Rose appeared suddenly beside me and asked "What happened? Is it serious? Did the code crash? You aren't the praying type. Are you ok?"

I sighed and muttered "Nothing". At the same time my mobile vibrated and signaled that a text was received.

I reacted in milliseconds by grabbing and unlocking the phone. I was trying to hide my disappointment when I saw the text was from a food chain giving out free coupons for burgers.

Rose immediately knew something was up when I reacted poorly for the free food announcement.

"Are you really ok? Are you dying?" She asked with real concern in her eyes. Trust her to be dramatic in the most normal situations.

"No, Rose. I am not dying. I am just tired of the burger." I tried to cover my tracks but nothing goes unnoticed in detective Rose's eyes.

"Nice try, Lexy. I will buy you a coffee and you will tell me all about it". She tried to buy me off with a coffee and it almost worked.

But we got interrupted by our boss. "Hey guys! Meet our new designer George. He is very talented and he will be working with us from today".

Oh, yeah. A new designer was supposed to join us today. I totally forgot. Can you blame me?

My brain had limited capacity storage and a certain somebody was occupying most of it without any rent. Let's shoo him away for a minute. Doesn't work like that, does it?

"Wow", Rose whispered to me. She was right. George was a good looking guy. But he was not as hot as you-know-who.

Dear brain, just stop it. Sincerely, me.

George was friendly and he mingled easily with all our teammates. Rose introduced herself and then turned to me. I said "Hi, I am Alex. A developer. Please let me know if you need any help".

George thanked us and left to talk with the rest of the team. What a nice guy! Unlike someone.

Dear brain, should I repeat myself?

After some time, George came back to my cabin. He smiled and said, "Really nice to meet you, Alex. I hope we could be friends. Can I have your number? I might need it for work and other stuff".

I nodded and said "Me too, George. Sure." He handed me his mobile to enter my number.

In few minutes, I received a message from him. "Hi! It's George". With smileys and all.

Look, that's how it works! Some people wouldn't know. No, I promised myself that I wouldn't think about it again. I gave him my number and why was I acting like a teenager with a crush?

He must have known I was thinking about him. If not, why would he text at the same time? "Yo! Baby! It's Dean if you haven't figured it out already" *winking emojis*.

Really? He had the nerve to send a late text and include winking emojis?

I stopped myself from replying immediately. He shouldn't know that I was waiting for his text. Not that I was. Ok who was I kidding?

I waited for an hour to reply and in the meantime I tried to think of a good comeback. Believe me, I really tried. I couldn't come up with anything other than "Hi".

So I sent it. Just a word. Nothing else. No emojis.

I immediately got a response. "Wow! No smileys? That's harsh".

I smiled upon reading his text and realized George came to my cabin to ask something and was staring at me now.

I was embarrassed and said "Hi George. Is there anything I can help with?"

"No, I just wanted to ask you if you wanted to get coffee with the rest of us but you looked, ahem, busy".

Suddenly my phone decided to show another text notification from "The Devil". That's what I named his contact. Cute, right?

It read "Coffee today evening @ the CJs. My treat. You in?"

George cleared his throat again. "I don't want to interrupt. Maybe next time".

I smiled apologetically and said "Sure". Then I texted Dean that I was in. He asked me to meet him at the cafe at 5 pm.

Why was I smiling? He said he was new in town and wanted company. It's not like he asked me out on a d-. Wait.

I needed to stop thinking right now. Was it a date? I didnt know. Did I want it to be a date?

Maybe.

Chapter 7

To say that I was nervous was an epic understatement of the century. I was excited and scared at the same time. It was going in the direction that I wished this relationship would progress. That was what scared me as well.

Was it really ok to be attached to a person whom I have met only twice and exchanged less than 4 or 5 texts?

Probably not. But when did anything about me made sense? You would not doubt my sanity at this point as we have crossed the point too long ago when I wrote my number on his hand. Heck, it went out of the window when I first saw him on that side of the highway.

He was doing this because he was interested too, wasn't he? You wouldn't ask a person you are not interested in to hang out in a coffee shop, would you?

But he was new in town and he could use a friend. Again, you wouldn't call a friend 'baby' or ask them to write in your hand, right? If you would, we need to have some conversation.

It was a date. Ok, maybe not. I was feeding my own delusional thoughts and I was not stopping anytime soon.

Would he be nervous too? Nah. It's impossible. He might have had coffee with random people on a daily basis. I wouldn't know.

Actually, coming to think of it, I didn't know anything about him other than his name and the fact that he was new in town.

Heck, I didn't even confirm his eye color. How would I describe him later to an officer of law?

Not that I would need to. Right? "He was really hot" would not be that helpful.

People usually get to know each other during coffee. I might have been inexperienced but I have heard things.

Getting a coffee. Opening the door. Pulling up a chair for the other person. How difficult could it be?

I should just go with the flow. I believe everyone has their own strength and weakness. Mine was over-thinking. Strength or weakness, you ask? I would say both.

He just wanted to get coffee and I was already light-years ahead in my thoughts.

"Muffin for your thoughts?" Rose waved her hands in front of me.

"Isn't it penny for your thoughts?" I was confused.

"Penny is not much of a bribe. Here, have a muffin. And tell me what are you analyzing with that head of yours? Don't tell me it's about work, I know that look."

"Nothing. Does getting coffee count as a date?"

"Depends. If you are getting me one, it's not a date. Are you getting me one now? If yes, grab me a cookie too. Sorry I am getting side-tracked. So who is this mysterious person? I don't get to meet them? Oh my god! Did you get another friend?" Rose gasped dramatically.

"Slow down Rose. Breathe. It's just someone I met the other day. He is new in town and wanted my help".

"Wow. And you kept it as a secret? That's suspicious. Is he hot?"

"I just didn't think it was that significant". I tried to avoid the "heck yeah" for the "hot" part but left it out for the reasons you could obviously guess.

She didn't look convinced but her mobile saved me. Someone was calling her. "I have to go now. I want all the details after your date". She said with a wink and left me with my thoughts.

"Not a date". I don't know why I bothered replying. She went in a hurry. Her boyfriend was picking her up everyday.

When I came outside, Rose and a guy were standing near the exit. That might be Jake. I haven't met him officially yet.

Rose looked at me and waved me over. "Sorry, I forgot to introduce you. Jake, this is my best friend in the whole universe, Alex. Alex, this is Jake, my boyfriend".

Jake shook my hands. "How are you doing, man? Rose told me so much about you. It's nice to finally meet you".

He seemed nice enough. "Likewise. Thanks for driving Rose to work. I am finally able to get some peace".

Rose punched me playfully and said, "He is just cranky because we are making him late for his date. Bye, Alex. Go get 'em, tiger".

"It's not a date. Anyway, I have to go. Bye, Rose. Nice meeting you, Jake". It was time to leave for my not-a-date.

When I entered the CJs cafe, Dean was already sitting on a table near the window. So much for opening the door and pulling up the chair. Wait, I could still buy coffee for him.

He wore a button down blue shirt with jeans. He probably styled his hair to look effortlessly cool. Ugh. Why was I so interested in how he looked?

He saw me and shot me a curious smile. I sat down on the chair opposite to him. "Sorry to keep you waiting. I was talking to my friend for a minute".

I didn't know why I needed to excuse myself as it was 10 minutes before 5, which was our agreed time.

"Hey, don't apologize. I am the one who is early. I didn't know how bad would be the traffic so I arrived before time".

I nodded and took the menu and started scanning the pages.

He looked sheepish and said, "Actually I have ordered coffee for both of us. I was sitting here without ordering and waitress was staring at me. So I felt guilty and ordered coffee. If you aren't ok with it, feel free to order something else".

I was sure that was not why the waitress was staring. I stifled a laugh and said, "No worries. I like all kinds of coffee".

He looked relevied. Was he really concerned about my choice of coffee? That was good to know.

The waitress came with our coffee and not-so-discreetly smiled at him and handed him a napkin with her number. He politely declined and she left with a pout.

"So, what would you usually do on a date?" He chose to ask this question right when I started sipping my coffee.

Chapter 8

"So, what would you usually do on a date?"

I started coughing violently as the coffee I was sipping lost its way and went to the wrong pipe because of his question.

He was looking at me with concern. "Are you ok?" He stood up and started patting my back.

"I'm ok. The coffee was a bit hot" I tried to look unaffected.

"Baby, it's a cold coffee" He was definitely stifling a laugh for my sake.

It had to be the most embarrassing moment of my life. You might think I'm exaggerating. Yeah, I wish.

"I was just making conversation. Don't take it the wrong way". He tried to explain.

"You ask personal questions to make conversation?"

"Sorry. I was just wondering. I feel like we have known each other for a long time". He said this with sincerity. I almost felt bad.

"Alright. Don't apologize. It's like we always keep saying sorry back and forth".

"Ok. So, back to the question. What do you do on your dates? What are the places you would visit? What activities do you like?"

So he might have just wanted to know the best date spots in this town. He might have asked someone out and wanted my advise. Thanks, dear brain. That didn't make me feel any better.

"I haven't been on any dates since I came here" I admitted.

"You have got to be kidding me. You don't date? Why aren't people lining up to ask you out?" He was really curious.

I stared at him like he grew two heads. He looked like he was genuinely surprised at my answer.

"Well. I don't know. I am a bit of workaholic. And you have seen my expertise in being so likeable. Come on! Not everyone is like you, probably going on dates on an hourly schedule."

"That's called stereotyping, Alex. To answer your questions, Yes, I am genuinely surprised. And no, I haven't been on a date either, it's complicated", he said looking down at his coffee.

Woah! Was he serious? I knew it. He was in jail, wasn't he? How else could you explain the lack of dates? But I kept that theory to myself.

"Really? Do you expect me to believe that? We have been here for 10 minutes and you have been already hit on by that waitress".

"Doesn't matter. I am not interested in her". He was looking at me with a strange expression. I didn't want to get my hopes up by trying to decipher some meaning out of looks like some expert.

Because let's face it, I couldn't predict the meaning of others' looks to save my life. Heck, I couldn't understand myself sometimes.

I was desperate for a topic change. "Nice coffee. How do you usually take your coffee? My most favorite is a latte with loads of whipped cream".

He smiled at my lame attempt to steer the conversation but didn't comment on that. "I like black coffee but I can get used to a latte too".

"Right. I don't know much about you. Are you from around here? What do you do for a living? Where are you staying now?"

He laughed at my series of questions. What can I say? I was born curious. Eventhough curiosity is believed to be a cat killer, it didn't discourage me to find out more about the man in front of me.

"Easy, tiger. I am not from around here. I am taking care of family business and I am staying at my condo at 11th street near the mall. You can come by anytime you want".

Wait, did he invite me to his house? That's 3 or 4 dates away, right? And this one didn't count. From what I have observed, he might not have even realized it could be interpreted that way.

He looked at me expectantly like he needed me to share something. I thought of answering the same questions.

"I am also here because of my job. I am working as a game developer at Dez. I am staying nearby the company. You can come by if you want. Um, when you are free. I can send you my location if needed". I have added the last part because he offered the same before.

"Really? I might take you up on that offer. How about this Sunday?"

I didn't expect things to be moving forward this fast. Was he coming to my house? I nodded with doubt but said "Sure".

He was smiling warmly and the waitress decided to come over and ask, "Do you need anything else?".

She was still sulking. Dean looked at me and I shook my head. He turned to the waitress. "No thanks. Check please".

Once she came back with the check, he grabbed it immediately before I could even react. Nice reflexes.

"At least let me share" I said and he looked at me like I asked him to kick a puppy.

"No, ba- Alex. It's my treat. I was the one who asked you".

"Fine. Next time I will pay". I realized that I said there would be a next time. "Uh, I mean, if we get dinner or something". Did I ask him on a dinner date? What was happening to me?

He voiced my thoughts. "Are you asking me out to dinner next time?"

"No. Yes. I don't know. Let's just say I want to thank you for the car incident and coffee".

"Sure, let's just say that". He was still smiling when we came to the parking lot.

"Thanks for the coffee. Do you want me to drop you off?" I looked around for his expensive car and couldn't find it.

He smirked and said, "No, today I didn't take my car. I felt adventurous so I took her". He pointed at something behind me.

"Her?" I turned around and I was not that surprised to see a motorcycle. I mean, look at him. Walking cliche, I know.

Let me tell you a little secret. I am a sucker for cliches.

Chapter 9

I stared at my screen. Did I see blue or green? I realized I didn't know the color of his eyes even after our coffee date.

Date? Yes, I would like to call it a date. Who cared anymore? I liked to live in delusion if you haven't already noticed.

I was pouting a bit as he bailed out on our plans by saying that he couldn't come to my house on Sunday. He had to go out of town to take care of an unplanned work.

I texted back, "Ok, drive safely". Let me tell you, I didn't feel like a kid whose ice cream was taken away. And as if that was the last ice cream on the planet.

Rose calling my name woke me up from my day dream. "Yo! Earth to Alex. You are not the same after your 'not-a-date'. Are you coming to dinner today with me and George? My treat. I invited Jake too".

I needed a distraction from the blue-green eyes so I accepted her offer. "Free food? Count me in".

Right after Rose went away, I got a text from Dean. "Are you free today? How about dinner?"

How could he do that? Was there some kind of bad telepathy? I was not the type to ditch my friends for someone I was not even dating yet. It felt weird to invite him along.

Rose would embarrass me or I would take up on that job by myself. I was not ready to bring him to my circle just yet.

I have already ditched George once to get coffee with Dean. I couldn't do it again.

Also, he bailed on me once. So it was my turn. You might think I'm petty, but I would call it as 'give and take'.

I replied "Shall I take a rain check? Made plans with friends tonight".

He replied immediately. "Ok baby, take care. Let me know once you get back home".

I was shocked to say the least. Was it normal wanting to know if your friends reach home?

"Okay" I tried to keep it simple. But the butterflies returned and stayed there for a long time.

The dinner was fun as we all were of the same age and discussed about many things after a little awkward beginning. Rose was the type who could bring people together and she was the life of any party.

I didn't remember how we became close. We were in the same college and then came to work in the same office. She was the opposite of me. She was protective of me like a sister and I loved her for it.

Jake was a decent guy and he took good care of Rose. George was friendly and matched Rose's energy level to keep the conversation going.

I was the introvert of the group and I liked to remain silent and laughed at their jokes and provided my valuable inputs occasionally. It was safe to say that I was enjoying myself with my friends.

Rose looked at me and said, "You are awfully quiet, Alex. Something on your mind? Or should I say someone?" So she finally decided to torture the information out of me.

I just glared at her and shrugged. "You know me. I am comfortable being silent".

George turned to me and asked, "You have met someone, right? You went for a date on the day I joined".

I shook my head. "No, it was just a friend".

Now Jake joined them. "Yeah, I remember seeing you going to meet your 'friend' in such a hurry".

"You too, Jake?" I tried to look hurt but my lips decided it was appropriate to smile at their comments.

Rose looked at my face and said, "Leave it for now, guys. We will find out soon anyway". This was why I liked Rose. She loved to tease me but she also knew when to stop.

"Alright". The guys surrendered and moved on to different topics.

Once dinner was over, Jake and Rose left together. George asked me if I could drive him home.

I have learned today that George was staying at a friend's place. I drove him there with his directions. He invited me in but I was tired so I told him I would come by some other day.

It felt normal and not like when Dean asked me to visit his home. I wondered why. Dear butterflies, where were you?

Then I drove back home and texted Dean. "I am back home now. Didn't try to make an art out of anyone's car today".

He replied few minutes later. "Haha. Very funny. Good night, baby. See you tomorrow".

Tomorrow? I couldn't recollect making any plans for tomorrow. But I wouldn't be surprised if my brain did something and kept it from me.

Chapter 10

"What did we plan exactly?" It was the only thought in my head when I woke up in the morning of the mentioned day.

Was I seeing him today? Where? Today was a weekday so I had to work. I didn't remember him mentioning dinner or coffee.

I thought of asking him but I just couldn't. What if he told that he sent it to me by mistake? What if it was meant for someone else? I was not ready to hear it.

I got ready and went to my office as usual. No point in getting dressed for an imaginary date. What if he didn't text me again today?

I was driving myself crazy with my own thoughts. You have been there. It wasn't exactly pretty, was it? Now imagine being there 24/7. Don't worry, I wouldn't even wish it on my mortal enemy.

Before I lost my mind completely, Dean called me. Was it the first time we spoke on phone? Must be a special occasion. He might even apologize for sending the text to me by mistake. Should I not pick up?

But I did. I had to. For my own sanity. "Hey! How are you doing? Is your day going well? I, uh, I believe I made a mistake. I realized it just now so I called. Hope I didn't interrupt your work".

I thought of telling myself "I told you so" but what was the point?

"Hello to you too, Dean. I am doing good. You didn't interrupt anything. I am just having lunch. What mistake?"

"I said I would meet you tonight. I thought about everything but it I forgot one important detail. Informing you of my plan. It's too late, isn't it? You might have already made plans, of course you would be busy". He chose not to let me talk and rambled on.

Wow. He was as forgetful as me. "Wait, Dean. I don't have any plans tonight. I rarely do. But next time don't forget to let me know beforehand. So that I can actually join you"

"Of course. Great. I saw a nice Italian place near your office. I checked the ratings and it has got 4.3 stars. Is it good enough or is there any other place on your mind?"

"Sure, I have been there and it's good. 4.3 stars rating is ok. But you need to be careful. If there are only a couple of reviews and the rating is 5, it might be the owner and his friends". What? I thought of sharing the wisdom.

"Oh, yeah? I will be careful next time. Anyway I can't believe I am getting for all those valuable advise for free". He couldn't hide the laughter in his voice.

"Fine, tease all you want. You would think about my words when you are having dinner at a restaurant and the owner of the place eating from a takeout container". I couldn't believe I came up with a decent comeback.

Ahh, I got it. This was because we were talking on the phone. Should I avoid meeting with him and talk only on the phone? What fun it would be without a little challenge of looking at his handsome face and not drooling?

"Fine. Shall I pick you up tonight? Will you be at the office?" He surrendered. Go, Alex!

"Yeah, but I brought my car. Shall I meet you at the restaurant?" Was he offering me a ride? Did I have to bring my car today? Sigh.

"Can you leave it at your office parking lot for a day? I want to give you a ride", He answered my un-asked question.

I knew it was time. I got used to having the butterflies inside my stomach. At this point, I might as well start naming them. How is Blaire for a butterfly name? "Ok. When are you coming?".

"I have a small errand and I will pick you up at 7. Be ready, Alex". Eventhough he mentioned it casually, I felt a chill on hearing my name. It felt like he was inviting me on a dare. I wasn't the one to back out.

Two can play this game. "Bring it on, Dean".

When I told my friends that Dean was picking me up for dinner, Rose wanted to stay and meet him. George was leaving and he said he wanted to stay but his housemate was sick.

Jake came to pick up Rose around 6 but she wanted to stay back and meet Dean. Jake said he made a reservation to celebrate their 1 month anniversary and apologized.

I really wanted Dean to meet my friends but that had to wait. I spent the remaining time doodling and playing games. I was counting the minutes.

Dean called me 10 minutes early and said he was waiting for me at the entrance. Thank god for his sense of timing as I was growing impatient with each passing second.

I saw him at the entrance and wondered whether I should go back and hide. You might be surprised by my sudden change of mind.

However, you would understand if you have seen what was waiting for me.

It was a motorcycle. Dean spotted me and asked me to come over. He had 2 helmets on his hand. He actually looked so cool like he could do a photoshoot on the spot.

I gathered my courage and walked towards him. He visibly brightened on seeing me and I would have appreciated if my heart wasn't beating erratically. As cliche as it sounds, I have never been on a motorcycle as I heard they were dangerous and I was a bit afraid to test that theory.

"Hi" I said breathlessly. He gave me a once over and said, "You look good. Nice shirt". I blushed at his simple comment and replied lamely, "You too".

He handed me a helmet and said "Hop on". I put on the helmet and stood on my spot. He must have sensed my discomfort. He squeezed my hands and said, "Trust me. You will enjoy it. If not, we can come back and take your car".

It sounded like a reasonable plan. So I decided to get on the motorcycle. Let me enjoy the thrill at least once in my life.

He took my hands and wrapped it around his waist. "Don't be shy and hold on tightly".

I nodded because I didn't trust my voice. I wrapped my hands around his torso. Was I hugging him? Before I could start looking for the butterflies, he took off.

Forget butterflies. It felt like hummingbirds and woodpeckers have taken over.

Chapter 11

I just had an amazing experience. I've got to tell you, Dean was a skilled rider. He didn't drive rashly. He was very conscious of our safety. It might sound boring but it made me enjoy the ride more.

My hands around his waist helped too. The wind was on my face. I couldn't hear anything other than the noise of the engine. It was therapeutic. I could imagine why some people were obsessed with their motorcycles.

I scolded myself for choosing a restaurant which was too close. The ride was short but I knew that this wasn't going to be the last time.

I got down and handed him the helmet. He was searching my face for any reaction. He looked visibly relieved when I smiled widely.

"That was amazing. You are really good" I complimented him sincerely.

His smile became more shy on hearing that. "I was really worried if I made a bad decision. But I am so glad that you like it. I can give you a ride anytime you want".

"Then expect my call often". I was still on that high.

"God knows that I already do. Let's go inside. It's freezing out here". I was surprised by his little confession. But I just nodded and followed him. Don't think I haven't done a happy dance inside my head.

When I was busy with choreographing my dance number, he walked ahead and held the door open for me and I thanked him. Did he steal my checklist for being a gentleman?

What was next? He was not going to pull up my chair, right?

Well, He did. I guess he referred to the same Wiki-How page on dating. No, I was kidding. I got it from a rom-com. Ok, fine. A daytime soap opera.

It really felt like a date now. This was the same restaurant I visited with my friends some days ago. But suddenly it felt so different. The atmosphere seemed romantic. Did they change the interior in few days? Not possible.

I was hyper-aware of that and wondered why I chose this restaurant instead of a safe place which is designed for a platonic hangout. Like the McDonalds or some small burger joint for which I still had a coupon.

I told myself I chose this place because I liked the food. Yes, that had to be it.

He noticed that I was quiet and voiced his concern. "Are you ok? Do you feel nauseous? Is it because of the ride?"

"No no. I am fine, really. Just thinking about the last time I came here with my friends".

"Oh, that's cool. Tell me about your friends. I want to get to know you".

Was he quoting from the soap opera now? But again, this was what people generally talk about on dates, right?

So I told him about my friends (I could use the plural because there were 3 of them) while ordering our food. Everything felt natural with him.

"Rose is your best friend and Jake is her boyfriend. George is your work friend, right?"

"Right. Rose is like a sister to me. I don't have any siblings of my own. Do you have any siblings? What about your friends?"

"I don't have any siblings. Actually I grew up in an orphanage. I have a guardian but no family members other than that. I have a few friends but no close ones".

He said nonchalantly but I felt bad for prying. "Sorry. You need not answer if you are not ok with it".

He dismissed my concerns with a wave. "No no. Don't feel bad about that. It is what it is. I have learned to accepted life as it comes".

He seemed really mature for his age. Wait, he said he took care of family business. I decided to ask him about that.

"But you said you are taking care of family business. No need to explain if you don't want to. I understand".

"My guardian is like my father. So I take care of his business. Next time I will tell you more about it. I am not in a mafia gang or anything. You can relax". He joked to lighten the mood.

"Actually I am disappointed a bit that you are not a part of mafia. I was looking forward to be a friend of a gang member".

He shook his head and laughed. His blue-green eyes seemed to light up every time he laughed. I was glad that I could make him smile like that. Woah! Where did that thought come from?

"On a serious note, you have me now. You can talk to me anytime, you know? I am not best at giving advise but I can recommend good series to watch and video games to play to forget your troubles".

"Thank you, Alex. I really mean that. You are awesome, you know?"

"You are just saying that because you have been eyeing my ravi-olis for a long time. Not going to happen, buddy". I tried to lighten the mood and it worked.

"You live upto your nickname, Don't you?" My mature response was sticking out my tongue. Well, I just proved he was not wrong.

We were eating in silence for a few minutes. It was not awkward or anything. It felt really comfortable.

This time I grabbed the check and threw a stern look at him. "My treat. I told you already that I wanted to thank you for everything".

He winked and said, "Ok, next time then". The waitress looked amused and left after giving me suggestive looks. I shook my head and laughed.

He drove me to my home. He insisted that he should come to my door to say goodbye. And I let him.

I opened my door and turned to him. "Thanks for the ride, Dean. See you around".

He stopped me by touching my arm and my heart stopped beat-ing. He pulled me into a hug and said, "No, I should be the one to thank you. For spending time with me and making me happy".

I patted his back awkwardly. Should I pull away after counting 3? Should I count with or without Mississippi? He pulled away after 5 Mississippis.

Was it normal or too long? I didn't know and I didn't have any experience to compare with. I just knew that it turned my legs to jelly and I loved it.

Chapter 12

After our dinner and hug, we met twice for coffee and once for breakfast. We went grocery shopping too. We kept finding excuses to run into each other.

I called him for breakfast because I was lazy to prepare my own. He called me for coffee as he was near my office and craved something hot. He came to the grocery shop near my home as he 'just needed to stretch his legs'.

One fine afternoon, I was knee-deep in my work and forgot to have lunch. It was another normal day at the office.

I received a text from Dean asking if I had lunch. I replied "no" and he immediately called me.

I picked up and he started to scold me without even a "hi".

"Are you trying to starve to death? It's 3 PM and you didn't have your lunch?"

"First of all, Hello to you too, Dean. Second, I am not starving. I ate a muffin, ok 2 muffins, during my break and I am still full from that".

"Muffins for lunch? Who are you, a toddler?"

"Hey! Don't hate on the muffins. Why aren't you at work? Why are you yelling at me instead?"

He seemed to calm down by then. "Sorry. I wasn't yelling at you. I want you to take care of your health. I finished my work early and thought of catching a movie. So I called to ask if you wanted to go with me".

"A movie? Sure, why not? I desperately need some time away from work. Shall I meet you at the mall?"

"No. The movie is at 8 PM. I will pick you up at your home, if you don't mind. It's been long since I drove you".

"Ok. See you at 7.30?"

"Sure, baby". It was a long time since I heard him calling me baby. I didn't realize I missed it until I heard it.

Wow! How was I going to survive our movie date?

I left for my home a little early and started getting ready. Should I even call it a date? We never explicitly mentioned that word to describe our 'hangouts'.

But hey, in my mind, I can call it whatever I want. Judge me and see if I care.

I decided against taking a shower as it might make me late. I changed my shirt and sprayed some cologne and prayed that I wouldn't smell bad.

I heard the doorbell around 7.20 and realized he was early as usual. I smiled at that thought and opened the door. My breath hitched as I saw him wearing a leather jacket and clutching a helmet at his hand.

He looked like he was just out of a cover of a cliched romance book I have read during my teenage years. Ok, I lied, that was yesterday.

The only thing missing was a bunch of tattoos. I wasn't sure if he had any. Not that I wanted to look. Wow! What started as an innocent thought escalated quickly. Abort! Abort!

"H-Hi. Do you want to come in?" He smiled as I stuttered.

"Are you ok, Alex? Do you have fever?". He touched my forehead gently and my heart suddenly decided to forget how to function.

"Yeah, no, just the cold wind". In my mind it sounded like a perfect excuse. He looked like he doubted me but didn't seem to question it further.

"Shall we go? The movie starts at 8 and I don't want us to be late". As expected from him.

"Sure. Let me lock my door".

I was skipping ahead as I looked forward to riding on his motor-cycle again.

"Someone looks eager to get on the motorcycle". He commented and helped me to put on my helmet.

"Yeah. As I said, it was great and I wanted to ride again".

I wrapped my hands around him which was like an added bonus. He took off and I got to enjoy the free therapy once again.

We arrived at the mall 15 minutes early and got our tickets for the "Warlord - the beginning of a saga". He insisted on getting the tickets so I bought a big tub of popcorn for us to share.

You could ask me why I didn't buy two tubs. But tell me honestly. You know the answer already, right?

The movie was good but being in a dark theater with him was like a torture. But in a good way. I was hyper-aware of his shoulders next to me.

Our hands collided multiple times thanks to the single tub of popcorn I bought. It was safe to say that the popcorn fulfilled its purpose. I felt the electricity each time I touched his hand but he looked relaxed.

He even went ahead and held some popcorn near my mouth for me to eat. I tried a pathetic attempt of a scowl to hide my surprise and he withdrew his hands with a smile on seeing my reaction.

My mind started spiraling and I started worrying at some point. Did he not feel the same?

Was I the only one imagining everything? What should I do? Keep my distance? I didn't think it was possible for me. I was already deep in it. Should I confess?

Chapter 13

The movie was over and I did not pay attention to half of it. We got up and started moving. There was a bit of crowd and I ended up clutching his arms so that we wouldn't be separated. He noticed that and smiled at me.

Oblivious to the storm brewing inside my head, he was talking about the usage of the ship as a metaphor for life. Was there even a ship?

I just nodded and added 'ohh's and 'hmm's whenever appropriate. He stopped abruptly and looked at me. "Are you really not feeling well, baby? Or the movie wasn't up to your taste? I'm sorry if I dragged you along"

God! I didn't mean to worry him. Heck it was not his mistake to be oblivious about my feelings when I didn't show it or tell him about it.

"No, Dean. Please don't apologize. It's not your fault. The movie was good but I was preoccupied by some work-related things. Really, I am fine".

He seemed to consider it for a moment. "Ok, next time, please tell me how you feel so that we can change our plans according to it".

"Sure". But I was not sure what he would do if I was honest about my feelings. Would he run away?

As cliche as it sounds, I didn't want to lose him. Did I want to hang out with him even if it was going to hurt me in the long run?

This was not good for my heart. I needed to keep my distance. I have yelled at many characters from books and movies for being dumb and not having the courage to confess and move on.

But once I was in the same situation everything the protagonists did made sense. But the difference was that in fiction their love interest would always return their feelings sooner or later.

But this was real life. He was not going to magically develop feelings for me. We weren't the protagonists, right?

He insisted that he would drop me at home so that I could get some rest. I nodded and got on his motorcycle.

The ride calmed me down somehow and I realized that I let the overthinking take over me and lost some precious time with him.

We reached home and he walked me to my door as usual. "Dean, I am really ok. Don't worry" I tried to convince him with a smile.

"Ok, Alex. I thought of taking you somewhere for dinner. But maybe next time".

Dinner. I completely forgot about that. "You want to come in? I can make some dinner for us". My mouth seemed to be disconnected from my brain. Temporarily or permanently? I didn't know.

"Really? That would be awesome. I mean that would be nice". He looked embarrassed at his choice of words. I chuckled at that and went inside.

He was looking around when I prepared dinner. My dinner was nothing fancy but reheating the leftover lasagna from the morning.

I asked Dean and he was more than ok with it.

I started whistling a tune while I prepared the table for our dinner. Dean heard it and started singing random lyrics for my tune.

"Yeah, baby! Cleaning the kitchen and putting the towels away! I can see you smiling so there is a way!"

"You didn't tell me you were a singer".I couldn't stop myself from laughing out loud. I noticed that I have been laughing more when he was around.

Stop. Don't make it awkward. I begged my mind. Dean made his way to the kitchen and asked, "Do you need any help?"

I told him that I got it and suggested him to watch some TV if he wanted. He was already comfortable like it was a regular occurrence for him to sit in my sofa and swiped through the channels.

He settled on a old cop movie and made small talk with me while the movie faded in background.

There was only one thought on my mind for the whole time. I could get used to Dean being at my home. There was a sense of comfort and warmth that he brought along with him. And I liked it. Maybe more than I should.

We had dinner and he complimented me on my cooking skills. I have told him the stories from my childhood and how I started helping my mom and learned cooking from her.

"So that's why the lasagne tastes so good. Is the secret love?" He teased me.

"I don't know about where to buy that mysterious 'love' ingredient but my secret is cinnamon".

"Now that I know your secret, do you have to kill me?"

"No, but my lasagne will take care of that". We both laughed and I felt lighter. See, it is easy to spew nonsense than to talk about real feelings.

He left after getting a call from his father. I was alone with my thoughts which was a dangerous thing for my sanity.

I started analyzing each word he said and every touch that happened. And I finally arrived at the conclusion that I had no clue how he felt.

Eventhough I could say that he liked spending time with me, I wanted to wait till I hear it from his own mouth.

Will he ever say it?

Chapter 14

When I heard the notification sound, I thought it was something my delusional mind came up with. Fool me a hundredth time, shame on you, brain.

But still my hand reached to grab my phone. Were any there part of me in my control?

"Thanks for the dinner and movie. I like spending time with you". It was from Dean. Was I seeing things now?

No, it seemed real. The pinch was really painful and I made a mental note to go easy next time if I wanted to check if it was a dream.

Can you tell me if I could stay sane after reading this text?

Was he planning to deprive me of my precious sleep? Nowadays I have been trading my game time for some quality sleep. But now I was going to stay up thinking about his words.

But I must have been more tired than I thought and fell asleep after few minutes of replaying the message on my mind. What did I think would happen? Would the message magically make sense?

I heard the alarm when I was dreaming something about Dean. Stupid clocks. I couldn't remember the dream exactly but we were on a campsite watching stars.

Should I go camping to distract myself? Should I ask Dean to tag along?

I decided against it so that I could hold on to the remaining shred of my sanity. At this point, you might need a microscope to even take a glimpse at it. My sanity, I mean.

I reached office and I could sense something was going on as people were animatedly talking among themselves.

Right on cue, our boss announced that we were having potluck lunch for the next day. We all needed to bring one dish each and to avoid repeating of dishes, each person was requested to bring a specific dish.

I opened the email which had the fateful list. I scanned for my name and it said 'cake' against it.

Sounds easy. Right? I could buy something on my way. But to my disappointment, something was written below. "This is a team building activity. You have to bring the one you made. If we find out it is store-bought, you have to buy coffee for everyone".

Wow! Were all the people in my office had a flair for drama? How in the world was I going to become a baker overnight? I have tried baking a few times before and it never turned out well.

Look at Rose, she got sandwiches and she was happy. Knowing her, she would buy it from the store and convince people that she even made the bread from scratch.

I heard a notification coming in at that moment and it was from Dean.

"Do you want to come over? I would like to cook dinner for you. You know, for yesterday".

"Are you taking revenge or something?" I replied immediately. I knew he didn't mean it that way. Still I liked to tease him.

"Your humor sense know no bounds. I am lol-ing. So, pick you up at 5?"

"Sorry, can't. I have to prepare a cake for potluck in my office tomorrow".

"Cake, huh? Need help?" He might know how to bake. He would at least help me buy one. I had to take his help, for obvious reasons.

"Yes, please. You can come to my house around 6 if that's ok". I told myself it was for the office. I wanted to make a good impression.

Just between us, I didn't really care about the cake. Don't tell my friends. I was happy that Dean was coming over. Again.

I was in the grocery shop near my home and looking frantically through a blog post which promised to teach baking to suddenly become viral overnight. Ok, hold your horses, blog people. Let me look for ingredients to buy first.

Why on God's green earth were these many types of cake? I didn't know which to choose.

No. The question should be, "Would people be able to eat it once I was done with the cake?"

Dean called me and I started complaining immediately. "How could someone learn baking and become viral overnight? God, I don't even know where to start. Should I choose dairy free and gluten free so that 'healthy people' could eat it? Can we call people healthy if they don't want to eat cake? What about vegans? I don't know everyone's preferences. I can buy from a shop but what if they ask me to buy coffee for everyone? I love my friends but they order expensive stuff if someone else is buying"

He was laughing like a maniac. Was I funny? I didn't intend to be. Not at that moment. "Baby, calm down. Breathe. Where are you? I will come and help you to buy things".

I told him that I was at the grocery store and he was there within 10 minutes. I was just picking random stuff and filling my cart until he showed up.

"Ready-made cake mix?" He raised his eyebrows. "Aww, you don't trust me? I'm hurt, baby".

"N-no. It's not like that. This is just a back-up. In case we need something extra". Did I offend him?

He poked my ribs. "Chill. I was just teasing. Keep it. Might help. I am not great at baking either".

We decided to buy the ingredients for a normal cake. Not vegan. Not healthy. Not anything. A simple cake. There would be other dessert options for people to choose from.

We checked out everything and we drove separately to my home.

It suddenly hit me that Dean would be in my home again. Baking a cake. Would the cake turn out good? Frankly, I didn't care. Would I do anything I might regret? Probably.

Chapter 15

"Have you ever baked a cake? 'Cause I have tried and it didn't turn well". I asked Dean when we were putting away the ingredients from our shopping trip.

"Yeah. Once. For my father. But he couldn't eat it so I ate the whole thing and got sick". He looked like he was remembering the incident fondly.

"Oh my god. I chose the wrong person to ask for help, didn't I? I don't want to get sick. But wait, this is for my friends. So let's do this."

"Haha. So why did you pick me?" He asked with a curiosity.

"For helping? I don't know. You were the one who offered". I answered truthfully.

He just nodded in an absent-minded way. Did I say something wrong?

I wouldn't have asked anyone else because I always liked to do things alone. Other people called it loneliness but I enjoyed solitude. But why was I letting him in and breaking my rules of solitudity? That didn't sound right. Solidarity? Whatever.

That awkwardness didn't last as he played some music and started to throw in lyrics that didn't make any sense. Take a look at this sample.

"I baked a cake with rainbow sprinkles.And danced with doughnuts, eating pickles.My oven sang a silly tune,While cupcakes landed on the moon!"

I was laughing until tears came out of my eyes. I was clutching my stomach and begging him to stop.

"Come on, baby. You know you like it".

I did. A lot. Instead I said "You wish".

He looked at me softly and said "I do".

I gathered my courage and asked, "What do you wish for?"

He considered that for a moment and grinned. "For now, the cake to come out good".

I groaned. Did I expect something else? Why did he do that when things get intense? He would make a stupid comment and change the topic.

"Baby, come on! Beat these eggs. We need to mix it with the flour".

Suddenly he was all business. I just couldn't read this guy. Maybe that was what kept me interested. Was that just an attraction? Curiosity about the mysterious guy?

I was not sure anymore. I thought of worrying about the cake first. I had all the time in the world later to analyze our situation.

He put on a playlist on his mobile and left it on the counter. He called it the "cake mix".

We worked without saying anything for a few minutes until the batter was ready.

He put the batter on the baking tray and set the oven timer. He turned to me and said, "That's it. Now we wait for 45 minutes". I was beginning to beleive that the cake would actually turn up good.

"Cool. I will clean up in the meantime. You can go and watch TV".

He said he would stay and help. I shrugged and began to collect all the used vessels to wash them.

He was packing the remaining flour in a container and decided it would be fun to flick some of it in my direction.

The flour landed on my hair and I was triggered. Food fight? Bring it on! I have seen people do that on movies and I remember thinking "Who would clean it up?"

But now I couldn't care less. I opened the tap and sprinkled some water on him.

He grabbed my hand to stop me from getting more water. His sudden movement startled me. And I ended up skidding across the floor and landed on my back.

Ouch, that hurt. It was not how I imagined things would go. Wasn't it supposed to be turn romantic? Who was writing the script? Could we talk?

Dean was shocked and he was muttering a string of curses. It was the first time I heard him curse and it was, um, hot. "Baby, I am really sorry. Did you hurt your back?"

I said I was fine and tried to get up. Dean gave me a hand and I winced when I got up. It was nothing serious but I felt some pain in my back.

"Don't strain your back. Let me help you". With that he lifted me like I weighed nothing and carried me to the couch.

"Dean! Put me down. I can walk". He didn't mind my pleas and gently sat me down on the couch.

"Can I lift your shirt? I want to check if there is any scratch or cut".

There was tension in the air and I didn't trust my voice to be normal.

I turned and he gently lifted my shirt and placed a finger at my back to check if there was any serious damage.

I just shivered at his touch. I didn't feel any pain so I thought I was in the clear.

"Dean, I am ok. Let's get the cake out and decorate it with something. Did we buy some sprinkles? Or chocolate chips? I think I have sy-"

I stopped rambling because I turned at that moment and his face was too close to mine. I could feel his breath on my face and it was minty.

He was staring at me. Or more precisely at my lips.

Was I dreaming? No, my dreams were never this nice. If it was a dream, I would be pissed if I wake up now.

Chapter 16

He was staring at my lips. But I had to open my mouth and say something.

"Dean?" I tried to get his attention but that came out as a whisper.

He looked into my eyes and I was melting from his smoldering gaze. "Dean? The cake?"

He was still not paying attention to my words. He needed to stop looking at me like that or I wouldn't be able to control my actions.

Did I say it out loud? He finally got out of his trance and realized our positions and backed away.

I was relieved and disappointed at the same time. Did I ruin the moment? Did I have to open my mouth and talk about the frigging cake? What would have happened if I closed the distance?

"Yes, cake. We need to take it out of the oven". He was looking uncomfortable. He added, "I stopped because I needed to discuss something with you. Not because I didn't want to. You know".

He was avoiding my eyes. What was it? I didn't care anymore. I just wanted to kiss him and confess how much I liked him.

But I stopped myself from doing all that because I wanted him to be comfortable and do things at his own pace.

I walked to the kitchen and opened the oven. My mind was fully occupied with the almost-kiss moment that I forgot to put on my oven mitts. I touched the cake tray with my hands and swore loudly.

Dean was there in a moment looking bewildered. He immediately took my hands away and held them in his own.

I felt calm at that moment. It was almost like a mirage and when I saw my hands, they were good as new. It was like I never touched the scalding hot tray.

I was puzzled and couldn't believe my own eyes as I kept looking at my hands. Dean was shocked too. He was looking like he was ready to console me if I started freaking out.

But I was not freaking out. I couldn't understand what happened but I trusted Dean. So much that it was almost scary. I was searching his face for any clues. What would he say after this?

"Baby, you need to use the oven mitts. Here". He put on the mitts and took out the tray. I decorated the cake, no, I poured some chocolate and sprinkles and decided it was enough. Who cared anymore? I would buy coffee for people in the next office too if needed.

He decided to break the silence. "Alex, you ok? You look a little pale. I can explain what happened. But can you give me some time? I don't want to lose you".

He didn't want to lose me? Me neither. I nodded. Let him explain when he could. It was not like he tried to kill me. In fact, it was the opposite.

"So the cake is ready. I believe people will like it if they get past the decoration. That's like the test of mental strength and those who pass gets the cake". I tried to lighten the mood but who was I kidding? The tension was still there.

He just smiled and excused himself. Was he leaving? I wanted to have dinner with him.

He looked like he was debating whether or not to stay. I wanted him to stay. I got a vote on that, right? It was my house.

"Dean. Stay for dinner. You have helped me and I want to return the favor".

He looked like he expected to get kicked out. "Sure. I will make dinner, then. You can rest".

I was not tired. I wanted to spend some time with him.

"No, I am fine. I will make dinner".

He sighed and proposed a compromise. "We can go out to get some dinner, if you don't mind".

"Ok. Let me get my wallet".

We rode in silence, which was unlike us. Usually Dean filled up the silence with his questions or songs. Or I did with my witty remarks. Don't roll your eyes. I can be funny when my stars align.

I decided to speak up. "Are you going to be normal or make this more awkward?"

"Huh? Sorry, Alex. I was distracted".

"Yeah, you were. Come on, let's not make this a big deal. Ok?"

"Really? I am wondering why you haven't kicked me out yet. I am just waiting for your shock to wear off. I am ready to jump out of the car if you say so".

"Ugh. Don't be dramatic. It's supposed to be my job. I won't kick you out. I am not in shock. I understand that something happened and you don't want to talk about it yet. You don't want to kill me or something, right?"

"God, no. It's the opposite. I just want to protect you".

"Ooh, I'm scared. I can take care of myself, Dean. I am 25".

"It's not that simple, baby. Please give me some time. I need to take care of something before I talk to you".

I nodded and then we stopped at the restaurant. We ate our dinner in silence. I kept stealing glances at him. He looked disturbed.

I felt like I couldn't do or say anything to help him. He had to figure this out on his own. I have made my decision and it was his turn.

We drove back in silence too. It was the most chaotic day but it ended in silence which I couldn't bear.

Chapter 17

After that day, I didn't hear from him for a week.

One frigging week. I was losing my mind. Was he kidding me? Can't he just text "good morning" or "have a nice day"?

But again, I didn't text him either. I didn't know what to say. I couldn't text him and say "Hey, remember me? You almost kissed me and then something happened and you ran away".

Was I not dramatic enough? No, that couldn't be it. God knows I can make any situation more dramatic than it need to be.

Was it such a big deal? Should I really freak out and run away?

Oh my god. Was I ready to do anything to make him like me? No. My self esteem was reasonably high. I felt insecure at times but no to a point that it would become toxic.

But I couldn't bring myself to be afraid of Dean. So what if he healed me by his touch? I was not a believer but I understand that there were things that simply can't be explained by Science. At least not yet.

I told myself to be patient. I was not known for my patience. It was not my cup of tea. In fact I was a coffee person. Right! Even my brain made terrible puns. No wonder he didn't text.

Rose came to me and asked, "Hey! Any plan for Valentine's? Jake is taking me out for a surprise dinner. Wait, how can it be a surprise when I know we are going for dinner? I guess it can be because I don't know where we are going." Trust Rose to answer her ridiculous questions on her own.

"Valentine's? Is it today? Ugh. No wonder the traffic was bad. It will be even worse in the evening".

"You are avoiding my question. What happened to Dean?"

"What about him? We are not in a relationship. He must be busy. Like all the others". It came out bitter than I intended.

"Come on. Did you ask him out? I know something is up. I can see the look in your eyes when you talk about him".

Rose always knew how to read my mind. "No, Rose. I have a deadline coming. I will deal with this later. You have fun on your 'surprise' dinner".

She patted my head and asked me to suck it up and talk to Dean. Then she left to celebrate the 'commercialized love day'. That's what I liked to call it.

George left to attend a single's night which wasn't my scene either. I was just waiting for the work to be over so I could leave for my house peacefully.

At that moment, my phone started vibrating like crazy and Dean was calling me.

My old butterfly buddies who went for a vacation were back with renewed energy. One call was all it took to make me feel like that? I needed to get a grip.

I tried to speak casually. "Dean! Long time no see. What's up?" I cringed at my own words.

"Baby? Are you free? Shall we meet?"

"You want to meet today?"

"Yes, today. Why? Do you have any plans?" He sounded genuinely confused.

I sighed. "It's Valentine's".

He was silent for a moment and said "Oh, do you have a date? I'm sorry. It's too late, isn't it?"

"No, you silly. Who would I go on a date with? I just thought that our usual places would be crowded".

"So, you don't have any plans? Amazing. No, I didn't mean it like that. I'm sorry. Let me start again. Do you want to come shopping with me? It's for my friend's birthday".

I chuckled at his comments. "Sure. Meet you at the gift shop?"

"Shall I pick you up at 5?"

"Sure, I would like that".

"See you soon, baby".

I was pacing nervously. I haven't seen him after our 'almost' moment. Would it be awkward?

He arrived 5 minutes early. Nothing has changed. He still looked dashing. I wanted to fix his hair. And before I chickened out and stopped myself, I moved his hair strand back in place.

He was shocked and flustered at the same time.

"Are you ok, Dean? I was just fixing your hair".

"No, Yeah. Um. You look nice today. Not that you weren't before. Ugh. What I am trying to say is, you look nice as usual".

Now it was my turn to be flustered. "Thanks. Where are we going?"

"There is a gift shop on the next street. But I have a confession to make. It was just an excuse to see you. Can we get some dinner afterwards? I need to talk to you".

I was taken aback by his honest words. "Sure. You can just ask to meet up. Why make up excuses? Anyway, Is it ok if we have dinner at my house? As I said, it will be crowded everywhere today".

"Yeah, works for me. Before I forget, here". He handed me a small box with a ribbon on it.

"What is it? I thought we were going to get some gift for your friend. Did you already buy it?"

"What? No no. This is for you. Happy Valentine's".

Chapter 18

All that things I preached about Valentine's being 'commercialized love day' flew out of the window when I saw that he got me a gift.

We went to the gift shop and he picked the first item that he laid his eyes on. Wow! Someone was in a hurry.

Then he drove us to my home. I asked him to sit on the couch and I brought two cups of orange juice. Dinner had to wait. Don't worry, I asked him and he was fine with it.

I saw his gift on the coffee table. "I didn't get you anything" I admitted while inspecting the box.

"No worries. I didn't exactly leave you on a good note. I was just trying to talk with my father before I could meet you again. I am thankful that you picked my call".

"So, did you talk with him? Wait. Shall I open your gift now?"

"Are you serious? No, open it later. And to answer your question, no, I couldn't get in touch with him. But I couldn't wait anymore. I had to see you and make it clear before you realize that you are better off without me". He said with a smile that didn't reach his eyes.

I could see he was only half-joking. It felt like he was really afraid of losing me. I could recognize that look because I was on the same boat.

"Ok. You know that I feel the same. What are we waiting for?" Here comes a moment of lost connection between my mouth and my brain.

He looked like he won a lottery and then lost it all on gambling. "Baby, I need to tell you something. You can decide if you feel the same after hearing me out".

I was sick of this game. "Unless you are a serial killer I don't think anything can change my mind" I confessed. Is that how people confess? "Like" word was not mentioned anywhere.

But he got the point. "You are really making it difficult to control myself. I want to do it the right way. Can you please wait?"

"Sure. I should warn you that waiting is not my strong suit. I could go out with the next person hitting on me". I said sarcastically.

His eyes turned dark at my comment. I felt a shiver down my spine. Did he think I was serious?

"Baby, you are not making it easy for me". Why was he holding himself back? I wanted to find out today. I didn't want to wait.

I know I sound like a baby. He called me baby so he was going to deal with one.

"Come on! You are not any better. You leave me for a week without even a "hi" and expect me to come running to you when you call me?" I asked knowing very well I did exactly that.

"Calm down, Alex. You know I was just being that way so you wouldn't get hurt".

"Hurt? I already told you, Dean. I am 25 and can take very good care of myself. Don't make my decisions for me".

"You really want to know? Can you promise me you won't run away?"

"If you haven't noticed, I was not the one who ran away".

I was not the one to speak like that but it seems that he had a deep impact on me. I didn't like being away him. Even for a week.

That realization hit like a brick and tears came out of my eyes without my permission.

He was stunned at my outburst and hugged me. "Shh, baby. Don't cry. I'm here. I won't leave you, ever. Even if you run away, I will find you and make you stay".

I wiped my tears and nodded. "Sorry. I think I kept everything bottled up for long".

"Don't apologize, baby. I was selfish and I didn't think how you would feel. But that doesn't mean I don't li-"

He stopped mid-sentence and placed a hand on his mouth. "It was not how I planned it to happen".

I was still in shock and didn't hear anything after that "li". He meant to say "like", right?

He liked me back? So what was stopping us? "Are you going to run away again?"

"No, baby. I promised I won't. Can you promise me the same?"

"Don't you need to check with your father before telling me any-thing?"

"Hypothetically, yes. But I guess he would understand".

At that time, I came back to my senses. "No, I don't want to jeopardize your relationship with your guardian. You can tell me later. I think I heard what I needed to hear".

"No, baby. I am ready now. I wanted to tell you when the moment is right. I think its now or never".

Chapter 19

I was looking at him expectantly. He took a deep breath and I did the same.

"Ok. So, What is your theory?" He was asking me to guess.

I was thinking for a bit and decided to keep it light. "Are you the devil? Because I might actually believe that." I said sarcastically.

He just smirked and said, "No, I am an angel. Your angel."

At that moment I knew there was no turning back. Who could have thought I would fall for a cheesy guy!?

Wait. What? I didn't even hear his story yet. He healed me with his touch. Did he mean it literally?

"Angel? Like with all the wings and stuff?"

"Well, technically, I am a human who is helping an angel. It's complicated".

"Then make me understand" was all I can say at that moment.

"I don't know where to start". He looked deep in thought.

"Just start from the beginning" I told him. Should I hold his hand?

As if he read my mind, he took my hand and entwined my fingers with his.

"Ok. Just like I told you, I was raised in an orphanage. My guardian was the one who was running it. I don't have any memory of my birth parents. My guardian told me they left me in front of his office".

I squeezed his hand reassuringly and nodded for him to continue.

"We called him father and he took care of us well. Me and a bunch of other kids. He loved us all and didn't make any of us feel left out. Once we graduated high school, many of my friends figured out their passion and moved out to pursue their dreams. I have volunteered to run the orphanage as our father had to be on the move most of the time. I didn't have any other plans for my future. So I decided that I could stay there and help him".

He continued after a little pause. "And he let me as I insisted that following his footsteps was my dream. When I was about 19 years old, he told that he was an angel. First, I didn't believe him. But when I stayed with him and observed him, I realized that he was telling the truth. He asked me if I wanted to be a part of his job".

"Job?" I wondered aloud.

"Yes, baby. You must have heard of guardian angels. They have the job of protecting the humans. My father is one of them. So I said I would do it but he asked me to wait and think carefully before making a decision. Once I was sure, he gave me a part of his grace to carry out the job".

My mouth had been open the whole time. I have heard stories but I never thought I would see someone like that.

"So I have the responsibility to look over few people who are little special. Like you".

"Few people? You do this with others too?" I was surprisingly a little jealous.

He started laughing. "Of all the things I said, you are asking whether I hang out with the others?"

"Of course. So why am I and few other people special?"

"Finally, a good question. It all goes back to your ancestors. My father was indebted to them in some way and they have asked him to protect their lineage in return. If something happens to you, it might affect my father's promise". He tried to keep it vague for some reason.

"So I am not in danger?" It's not like I was in a gang or something.

"No, baby. No one will hurt you. I promise. This is just my father keeping his word. Listen, it's a long story and I don't want you to be overwhelmed right now". It was his turn to squeeze my hands reassuringly.

"Usually, guardians don't mingle with their subjects. But when I observed you from afar, you were so adorable and I just couldn't get enough. So I broke the rules to talk to you. I could have just sped away after the car incident but I wanted to take a chance".

He did what? "So, what can you do with your powers? Are you immortal now? Will you never age? No, you said you were about 19 when it happened. You don't look 19, no offense. Sorry I am rambling".

"Baby, it's ok to be shocked. I can help people with my power, at least to some extent. I will tell you everything later when I have more time. I am still human so I am not immortal. Yes I don't look 19 'cause I am almost 26".

"Ok" I was lost in my thoughts. Everything was a tangled mess in my mind.

"You are freaking out, right? I shouldn't have said anything. I understand if you want me to leave. But I promise that you are not in danger".

"What? No, I am not freaking out. Well, may be a little. But I don't want you to leave. You can stay, if you want, of course".

"Ok, you can take your time. You can ask me anything but you need to rest for today. I am not going anywhere. We have all the time in the world".

I liked the sound of it. I smiled involuntarily. "Sure, do you want to stay for dinner?"

"Sorry, baby. Can I take a rain check? I want to look for my father. As you can guess, he doesn't use his phone often. I left a note with his friend. I have to wait at my place in case he decided to visit today".

I nodded and he gave me a hug before he left. I missed him already. I knew it was going to be a long night.

Chapter 20

When the alarm rang on the next day, I couldn't get up because I could swore I went to sleep just 10 minutes ago.

I didn't have a choice but to wake up and go to the office.

"Should I take a sick leave? And tell them what? An angel made me sick?" I was talking to myself while the phone rang.

It was not who you thought it was. You didn't think that? Fine, I did. No words from him yet. A "good morning" text would be nice. Should I send him one? When did I start to worry about texts? Ugh!

It was Rose. She shouted "Hey! Did I wake ya?" before I could say hello.

"No Rose, but you might have woken up my neighbor. What's up?"

"Haha. There, I laughed. Can you pick me up today? Jake said he was going out of town".

"Sure. I will pick you up at our usual time then". I missed hanging out with her. With all the relationship stuff, we couldn't spend time like we used to do.

I thought of getting ready and the phone rang again. Without noticing the name, I picked up and asked, "I said I would pick you up. What now?"

The deep chuckle didn't belong to Rose. "Good morning to you too, sunshine. Should I be jealous now? I thought of picking you up for breakfast but you have already made plans?"

"Oh, sorry Dean. Rose called me just now. So I thought it was her again. Yeah, I said I would pick her up today. Do you want to come along and meet her?"

"Sure. Are you ok with that?" He asked.

"Yeah. She has been nagging me to introduce you for a while now. Can you pick me up at 7.45? Then we can meet Rose".

"Ok, see you then, baby".

"Ok" I said and there was a long pause.

I thought of hanging up and then he said "I missed you. I know I saw you yesterday but I just felt like saying it".

"I know. Me too. Now go get ready. I will see you in an hour". I was now eager to get ready.

After an hour I heard the doorbell and I rushed down to open the door.

He was standing there with a flower on his hand. I couldn't believe it. Who thought he could be such a romantic person?

He rubbed the back of his neck and said "Here". He looked so adorable at that moment and I restrained myself from pinching his cheeks.

"Thanks, come on in". I went inside to put the flower in some water.

When I came back, Dean had a box in his hand that looked familiar. It was the gift that he gave me yesterday. Was he taking it back? Should I have said "no backsies"?

"You were very eager to open the box yesterday but then forgot about it completely?" He was shaking his head at me and smiling.

I looked at him sheepishly. "You asked me to open it later. Then you dropped a bombshell on me and went home. How do you expect me to remember?"

His expression changed and I felt guilty. "Sorry, baby. I was waiting for my father and he didn't show up. I will make up to you, I promise".

"Hey, don't apologize. I was just making excuses for forgetting it. I am opening it now". I took the box from his hand and opened it.

There was a small ring. It had two wings and a red stone in the middle. I raised my eyebrows at him. "Isn't it too soon?"

He just laughed and said "I saw this and thought it would be a reminder of the day that I confessed to you. Good that it was on Valentine's. More ways to remember. Try it on, baby".

I did and it fit me perfectly. I loved it. I didn't want to take it off. "You have great eye. I like it". I wiggled my fingers at him to show off the ring. He caught my hand and placed a small kiss.

I was surprised at his action. My hand was tingling and don't even get me started on my heart. It was going thousand miles per second.

"It looks good on you, baby. Now let's go before I change my mind and ask you to stay".

I wanted to stay too. But I promised Rose that I would pick her up. And she would be happy to finally meet Dean. So I just nodded and followed him to his car. Yes, the one I saw on the first day I met him. It seemed like it was only yesterday.

Time does fly fast when you are with the right person. Me? I am sure that I have found the most romantic one!

Chapter 21

The drive was short before we arrived at Rose's house. She couldn't recognize the car so I rolled down the windows and called her.

She was surprised and came running to the car. "Wow! You didn't mention you were coming with your boyfriend. He is as handsome as you described"

"Rose! When did I say that? Stop embarrassing me". I started blushing at her words.

Dean was just smirking. "Ba- Alex, you never said that to me". He turned to Rose "Hi! I am Dean. Great to finally meet you! I have heard a lot about you".

"Nice to meet you too. Alex kept you as a secret. But I can see why" Rose winked at me and I rolled my eyes.

"Stop, Rose. I am begging you". I didn't want to be the center of a conversation. Classic introvert problems.

Rose decided to leave me alone and made small talk with Dean.

We went to get breakfast at a cafe nearby. Judging by the way Rose was observing us, I thought she might want to present her findings later.

Rose and Dean got along well and that made me happy for some reason. She shared some of my college stories which mortified me. But Dean was enjoying it so I didn't mind. He already knew all of my quirks. Why start hiding now?

After breakfast Dean dropped us at the office and he left. I let him go because he promised to pick me up on the evening. I turned to Rose and she was looking like she wanted to say something. "What?"

"You are in love, Aren't you?" Trust Rose to come straight to the point.

"No. Maybe. I don't know, Rose. I don't have any experience to compare. I feel good but it's complicated. I am not sure if I am allowed to date him. I don't know if he feels the same and it scares me, Rose".

I took a deep breath. It felt free to finally talk about it with some-one.

"Wow! It must be the first time you said this much in a conver-sation. I am proud that little Alex is growing up" She pretended to wipe the imaginary tears from her eyes.

"Shut up, Rose. Thanks for your valuable input" I said sarcastical-ly.

"See, that's the Alex I know and love. Seriously though, you don't need to worry. I can tell he feels the same about you. Even more, if I dare say. It might be cliche but follow your heart".

"I know it's not like me but I just want to go with the flow. I don't want to over-think and lose him, you know?"

She nodded and gave me a hug. "You know you can talk to me anytime, right? Let me know if he breaks your heart. I will damage his expensive car". Rose said sincerely and I smiled at her.

"Thank you, Rose. I know that" I replied and then we went on our separate ways.

When I was working, George came to talk to me. "Hey Alex. I saw you and Rose with someone today morning. You did the boyfriend introduction and forgot to include me?"

"Did Rose set you up to this? No, he is not my boyfriend. He was just dropping me and Rose. I will introduce you when he comes today evening. Happy?"

"I haven't talked to Rose yet. It was my own observation. By the way, I want some help with the presentation. Can you come with me, please?"

With that, we got into our work mode and forgot about the rest of our world. Did you believe that? Good. 'Cause I didn't want others to know how much I was missing my not-a-boyfriend.

I looked at the clock today more than I had in my entire life. Never knew that the simple words "I am here" could make me euphoric. Ok, don't leave yet. I am not that dramatic, ok?

I called Rose and she told me that Jake was back so she would wait and go with him. George was busy with his presentation and he said he would meet "my friend" next time. The quotes were his and not mine.

Did that mean I was going to be alone with Dean? How was I supposed to behave in these type of situations? I honestly didn't have a clue.

Chapter 22

E vening came later than I would have wanted and when I came out of the office, Dean was standing there leaning on his motorcycle. My eyes appreciated it but that was not a good thing for my poor heart.

I waved at him and he smiled back. He also seemed nervous but I couldn't figure out why. Then it hit me. This might be his first time too. He didn't mention having any exes, Did he?

"Hi, um, y-you look nice". You thought it was me who said it, right? Wrong. He must be more nervous than he let on.

"Hey! I am sure I look like a zombie after a day of work. Are you ok?" I was genuinely worried.

"I am fine. It's true. You always look nice, baby."

"Y-yeah, you look ho-nice too" I almost said "hot". I didn't expect him to compliment me so I lost it momentarily.

"Ho-nice? Always say what you think, baby. At least to me" He winked at me.

I felt the blood rushing to my face. I decided to be honest. I liked the feeling. "Ok, you look hot. Happy?"

"Very much so. Let's go, baby. I am starving. Also I think I owe you few answers".

I was happy to ride with him in his motorcycle again and I was getting so used to it.

We reached my home as I wanted to have dinner with him some-place quiet. I just had a couple hundred questions.

But he chose to ask me first. "What is your ideal first date?"

"Slow down, cowboy. Shouldn't you ask if I want to go on a date with you in the first place?" I teased him.

He placed a hand on his mouth and gasped dramatically. "So you led me on and now friend-zoning me?"

"Come on! How can I assume things on my own? You have to say what's on your mind too".

"Baby, I thought my feelings were evident from day 1. As I told you, I broke the rules by talking to you. I like spending time with you. Now if it's ok with you, shall we go on a date?"

How could I say no to him? "Yes, Dean. I would love to. Now, to answer you question, I don't have any preference. But I love to go camping. We can go there, if you want. I mean, if not, we can go to movie and dinner".

"We already went to movie and dinner. So those count as well?"

"Um, no, I don't think so. We went as friends, right? So those do not count. I don't know. Does it matter? All I want is to be with you." Did I always have to make it cheesy? He didn't seem to mind.

He was surprised and he held my hands. I suddenly felt shy and looked at our entwined fingers.

"To be honest, it doesn't matter to me either. I mean, I have liked you from the beginning and my thoughts were not as innocent as a friend during those times".

Wow! This was how I was going to die. His words made me so excited and I was afraid my heart was going to jump out.

I suddenly made an impulse decision and kissed him on his cheek. My brain registered what I did a second later and I started freaking out. Did I cross a line? Why did he become still like a statue? Was he ok?

He touched his cheek and looked like he couldn't believe what happened. "Baby" he whispered.

I was so embarrassed by my own action and hid my face with my hands. He pried my hands away.

He placed his hands on my cheeks and looked into my eyes. "Baby, look at me. Don't feel shy with me. I was just surprised. In a good way. I love it when you are being like this".

I just nodded at him and excused myself to make dinner. He came along with me to help. That's what he said. But he started munching on the carrots I was cutting for dinner.

He tried to take another and I swatted his hands away. But he took a piece of the carrot and placed it on my mouth. Before I could register what was happening, he took a bite from the other end of that small piece.

His mouth was mere inches from mine. I was shocked and the carrot fell from my mouth. He picked up the piece and threw it on the dustbin muttering "Such a shame".

Wait. What happened? What was he trying to do? Was that another almost-kiss?

Chapter 23

After the almost-kiss, I made dinner in shocked silence. He was smiling and singing like nothing unusual happened.

Did I want to kiss him? Yeah, sure. But I didn't know why I freaked out. What would have happened if I didn't drop the frigging carrot?

I shuddered at that thought. Was I making it awkward? Right on cue, he came into the kitchen and looked at me. "Baby! Are you ok? You are awfully quiet. Did I make you uncomfortable? I am sorry. I was just playing around. I wouldn't do anything you don't like".

Was he for real? I was not a saint either. I had feelings for him too. "Don't apologize, Dean. I was the one who kissed you first. I was just shocked as this is all new to me".

"Do I look like someone who does it a lot? This is my first time as well. I just follow my heart when I am with you. I want you to do the same".

So was he my boyfriend? "Ok, shall we have dinner? I am dying to ask you some questions".

"Sure, baby. I will not leave today without answering you".

We had dinner while watching a reality show. He yelled at the contestants when they didn't know simple answers. It was endearing to watch. He was like a kid at that moment.

The more I spent time with him, the more I liked him, if it was possible.

Once the show was over, he switched off the TV and turned to me. "Sorry I got carried away watching that. You told me you had few questions. Ask away, baby".

I had too many questions but at that moment my mind was blank. I was thinking how close we were and how his eyes had the most confusing blue-green color.

I tried to blurt out the first thing on my mind. "Are we in a relationship now? Are you my boyfriend? Are you allowed to date? What if your father isn't happy with you and decided to punish you or something?"

He shook his head. "Calm down, baby. I don't know if I can date yet. I have chosen this life. But I am sure I can find a way to be with you. So if you are ok, then I am your boyfriend".

"I am more than ok. I don't want you to give up on helping people as you have told me it is your passion. But I am afraid you will break up with me if your guardian says so".

"No, baby. I won't do that. I will not be the one to break up with you if someone says something. I am not selfish and I will not leave you to deal with it all by yourself. I will always stick around and keep you safe until you get tired of me".

"Then you should be warned. I will not be tired of you. Ever".

"Bring it on, baby. I am ready to prove it to you". I felt safe and at ease with him.

"You told me you came to watch over me. How long has it been? But I haven't seen you".

"I don't know how much I can tell you, baby. But trust me, you will never be in any danger. At least not when I am here. You might not have seen me as I have been with you for less than 3 months. We take turns every year to watch over a human. This is to avoid getting attached to someone. But that didn't work for me as I fell for you very soon. I have been doing this for the past 5 years and I have never felt this way. You changed me baby. You make me feel things I never knew existed in the first place".

Tears were falling from my eyes on hearing his lovely words. What have I done to deserve his love? He was the one who looked over me. I voiced that thought. "But I haven't done anything for you. I almost hit you with my car".

He wiped my tears. "As you said, it was partially my fault for cutting you over. I was worried about you and wanted to make sure you were ok. You don't need to do anything. Having the opportunity to get to know you is the best thing ever happened to me. I have always looked after people. So I thought it was the same thing. But it's different. I want to be selfish and keep you with me always".

"I have never felt this way either. And I am not as good with words as you. So I just want to say that I like you. More than you would think. More than I have liked anyone else".

"That's enough for me, baby". He held my hands and squeezed my fingers.

I was trying to stifle a yawn but it escaped anyway.

"Did I bore you to sleep?" He was amused.

"God, no. I just had a long day at the office. Do you have any questions for me?"

"Yes, just the one. Why are you so adorable?"

"Why are you so cheesy?" I retorted.

"Don't pretend that you don't like it". Dang, he was right.

"Ok I give up" I surrendered.

"That's my baby. Go to sleep. I am leaving now. I have to wait for my father again. I will pick you up for office tomorrow".

"Good night, Dean". I walked him to the door and he stopped to look at me.

"Good night, baby". He pressed a kiss on my cheek and rushed to his motorcycle. He must have sensed that I was confused and explained "I might not leave if I stand here for another second".

Who wouldn't love him?

Chapter 24

As soon as I woke up, I felt myself smiling for no reason. Ok, there was a reason. Because my alarm was replaced by a message tone with a cute message "Morning, baby! It's coffee time!"

Sigh! Will I ever get used to this? I sent a quick reply asking him to come over for breakfast.

I was excited to see my boyfriend. I was just repeating it in my mind so I could remind myself that it wasn't a dream.

When I opened the door later, he was dressed in a casual jeans and white t-shirt but still managed to look like he came straight from a runway.

"Baby, are you going to let me in or you want to keep looking?" He teased.

I wanted to tease him back but I didn't have any good comeback. Are you even surprised at this point?

So I pulled him inside by his hand and pushed him to the wall and placed my hands on his sides. "I can check out my boyfriend, right?"

He looked stunned for a second and pulled me closer by putting a hand around my waist.

It was my turn to he shocked. I didn't plan this but I didn't want to stop.

"Do you not want to go to office today? You are putting me in a difficult position here". His breath was close to my ear and it tickled.

I felt heat rushing to my cheeks. I moved back and looked at him. "I just wanted to tease you. I want to go to office. I have a lot of works to complete. You know, the deadline is tomorrow for the big project. We are yet to complete the testing. I am not even sure if everything works. What if it crashes?"

"Baby, calm down. You are spiraling. I am sure you would have done a great job."

"Sorry. I was a bit nervous. Come in, let's have breakfast". I was wondering if I spoiled the moment.

"Don't apologize, Alex. You can talk to me about everything. You look cute when you ramble. Also, I love it when you open up. That's one of my perks of being your boyfriend".

I felt shy on hearing that. "Thanks, Dean. I am not sure if that was a compliment, though".

"I love it when I make you blush. I love it when you smile at me. I love many things about you and I always want to hold you like this". He was looking into my eyes. If I heard it from someone else, I might have thought it was cheesy.

But I wanted to freeze that moment and record his voice in my head so that I could replay it whenever I wanted. That would be a cool feature.

"Can you say that again so that I could get it on video?" I asked him and he started laughing.

"Baby, You are the only one who could think of something like that. Anyway, I can record it and send it to you. Should I go top-less or will you get distracted?"

"Wh-what? Sure, I mean no. I, uh, I just thought it was beautiful and wanted to keep it forever. But on second thought, don't do it. It would not be the same".

"Don't worry, baby. I will keep saying stuff like this until you get tired of me. I feel like I have no filter around you".

Wasn't he the sweetest? I kissed his cheek and said, "This is for being the best boyfriend".

"Come on, baby. Let's get you to the office. I might ask you to stay here if you keep doing this".

Wait, I felt like I forgot something important. "Right. I forgot to ask. Did you meet your father?"

"That was what I was going to tell you before you distracted me. I am not complaining, though. Yes, I saw my father yesterday and told him everything".

I tensed up on hearing that. What did he say? Dean was in a good mood, so nothing bad could have happened, right?

"Relax, baby. My father was cool with it. I asked if he was not shocked and he said and I quote, 'You think you are the first one to fall for a human you are supposed to look after? Get over yourself'. So, I think its safe to say that we are official now".

"Official now? So you would have ditched me if your father said so?" I tried to joke.

He poked my ribs. "Baby, you know I wouldn't. You can't get away from me easily".

"I don't want to". I winked at him.

"Look, my baby is all grown up". He pretended to wipe his non-existent tears.

I slapped his arm playfully. "Let's go, Dean. I don't want to be late".

"Before you go, I wanted to ask you something. Do you want to go on a date with me?"

"Our official first date? Ye-yeah, cool. Awesome. I mean, sure".

He chuckled at my pathetic attempt to hide my enthusiasm. "Ok baby. Let's go somewhere this weekend. Sounds ok?"

I nodded, not trusting my mouth anymore. After breakfast, we left my home.

We held hands throughout the ride despite my protests about safety. He said it was fine since it wasn't me who was driving. Angels could be sweet and arrogant at the same time.

Chapter 25

The week went by quickly as I had my work occupying the major portion of my mind.

I went for 3 days without proper sleep, not that it was new for me. But Dean was concerned and threatened to kidnap me from my office.

I convinced him that I would take rest at the office whenever I could. He kept himself updated on my food and sleep habits through regular calls and messages.

Being cared for is the best feeling in the whole wide world. You are welcome to debate me on this.

Rose was busy with her own tasks so I worked with George for this one. He was being nice and offered me help whenever needed.

Everything was over on Friday and the team planned to celebrate by going out on the evening. But I excused myself as I already made plans.

Dean was waiting for me in front of the office as he promised.

He looked alarmed when he saw me. It must have looked like a zombie-vampire crossover happened on my face.

He pulled me into a hug. "I missed you so much, baby. I thought I would go crazy if I didn't see you tonight".

"Me too" I tried to say but that was interrupted by a huge yawn.

"Come on, baby. Let's go home. You must get some rest. At least in the weekend".

"But what about our date?" It was the one thing I was looking forward to the most. It motivated me to finish my work within the week itself.

"Don't worry about it, baby. We can go once you are well-rested. I have already planned something." He held my hands and assured me.

We had dinner near my office and I fell asleep on the way to home.

When I woke up, I was on my bed and Dean was holding my hand. He was also sleeping next to me. He must have carried me to my bed as I didn't remember waking up.

I was wondering if it was a dream. I touched his cheek and he stirred a little but didn't wake up.

I wanted to look at his face and memorize all the details. Don't ask me if I was going to draw him later. No, I couldn't draw to save my life.

He looked so calm even in his sleep. Is it creepy to watch your sleeping boyfriend? Yes? Maybe? Who made the rules?

He had this calm aura even when he was awake. Was it because of his angel-ness? Wait, was it even a word?

"Angel" I whispered. I still couldn't believe it. Everything is just a story until it happens to us.

"Baby, you need to wipe that drool off your mouth. It's so obvious".

He woke up and chose teasing. I instinctively checked the corners of my mouth for any drool. What? It might have happened during deep sleep and not during the un-creepy checking out of the sleeping angel.

I slapped his hand. "You are the one with the drool. Oh, and don't think I didn't hear the snores". Two can play this game.

"Baby, I know you like me too much to care about my drool and snores".

Was he so full of himself? Yes. Did I love that? Heck, yeah.

I flicked his forehead lightly. "No, I care about my pillow covers more. Now, wake up. Let's get some coffee".

He just wrapped his hands around me and pulled me towards him. "Baby, 5 more minutes".

My heart was beating fast. I was conscious of my breath. Should I have brushed my teeth before I decided to poke his face and wake him up?

"Baby, you can be yourself when you are with me. Don't hide or try to change anything. I like you the way you are. Bad breath and all."

"Can you read minds?" I was too shocked. How did he know?

"What? No. I saw you trying to smell your breath. You are so adorable."

I punched his stomach lightly. "I am going to prepare coffee. Go take care your stinky breath and join me."

"Ok, baby". I got up and made coffee for both of us. I took a cup and went to the porch to enjoy the view while sipping my coffee. It was my morning routine.

I felt a hand around my waist and saw Dean with a coffee cup in one hand. It felt surreal to be here with the person who made the morning coffee even better.

"So, what is the plan for today? Do you need to go out for work?" I asked him.

"Yes, but I will be back in the evening to take you on a date. If that's ok with you. How are you, by the way? You look better, baby".

"Yeah, I am fine. We can go on the date. Where are we going?"

"It's a surprise, baby. You will see". He was smiling and it was contagious. I found myself smiling even more widely.

"Baby, Can you call me like how you did today morning?" He was a bit hesitant.

"What? Stinky breath? Drool face? I don't remember." I loved playing with him.

It didn't faze him. He was looking at me expectantly.

His look broke my resolve to tease him more.

"Angel". I looked into his blue-green eyes and I couldn't bear it so I looked away.

He turned my head towards him and said, "I really love it when you call me that. You don't know how much I like you".

"I like you a lot too. Now go finish your work early and come back soon".

"Yes, boss. I will be here by 5 PM. Wear something warm, baby".

He pecked my cheek and left me alone with the butterflies, my trusted old buddies.

Chapter 26

I won't bore you with details of how I chose my outfit for the date. Let's say Rose won't pick up my calls for the rest of the evening and I have a lot of clothes to fold once I am back from the date. I settled on a flannel button down with my blue jeans and threw on my favorite red sweater.

When I heard the doorbell at 4:55 PM, I was so nervous and excited at the sane time. I felt strangely calm when I opened the door and looked at my boyfriend. The one who was taking me on a real date. I have been skeptical of relationships and made fun of my friends when they were love-sick but look at me now!

It's like I was trapped in a city of love epidemic and voluntarily got infected. You would think these cheesy lines too, if you take a good look at the guy waiting at the door.

If you have come this far, you would know Dean wouldn't disappoint us in the looks department. I was a little shocked to see a hint of nervousness in his face and I felt so glad to find that I had that effect on him too.

He looks cute with a carton of eggs in his hand. Wait. Did they change the rule about the gifts you give before the date? And no one thought of telling me?

"Baby, you look good. Are you ready for the date? Here, take this first". He gave the carton of eggs to me.

"Dean, don't take this the wrong way. I am not sure which website you got your idea of gifts from, they might not be legit".

He laughed out loud and I loved that sound. "I noticed that you used up all the eggs while making breakfast today so I thought of restocking. But I love how your mind works. Sorry, I didn't get you flowers. I knew I missed something".

I was touched that he remembered such a trivial thing like that. "Don't be sorry. I was just kidding. I love this more than the flowers. Do you want to come in?"

"Do you mind if we leave right away? I don't want us to be late".

"Late? Are we going to watch a movie? Can you please give me a hint?"

"No, we aren't going to a movie. I don't want to spoil it. Come on, baby. Let's go!"

"Fine. Don't ask me to wear a blindfold though" I said with a sigh.

"Not now, may be later" He winked at me and I slapped his hand wondering how my mind got so dirty so soon.

We took his car and soon we were driving away from the city. There was a small hill on the outskirts and I never went there till now. Dean stopped and parked his car in a clearing near the top of the hill.

"The sunset here is wonderful. I come here often just to watch it. I wanted to watch the sunset with you from the moment I saw you. I have never brought anyone else here. Please tell me if you don't like it or if it feels boring. We can go to a movie or something like that.

God! I should have planned better. It's not so exciting, is it. It felt so romantic in my head, geez"

I was awestruck. It was the most romantic moment and I had to do something before he lost his senses from all the rambling.

I closed the distance and pressed my lips to his. He was shocked for a second but then he started kissing back. My eyes closed as if they were told to do so.

I don't want to use the clichéd firework analogy but it feels wrong not to. I could swear I felt some electricity at some point.

His lips were soft and demanding. It was everything I could ask for in a kiss. My hands had a mind of their own and sneaked up to his neck. And I felt his hands on my sides holding me so closely.

He tasted like cupcakes and cotton candy. I didn't know how he pulled off that combination but if someone could, it would be him.

I lost it when he licked my lower lip. I might have made some sound which brought us back to this world. He backed away a little bit but didn't let go of me.

When I opened my eyes, he was looking at me with hooded eyes and I blushed like there was no tomorrow. I blamed it on the cold weather. But it was hot there for some reason.

"Um, that was, well, amazing. Was it ok for you?" He was adorable that I wanted to kiss him again.

"Ok for me? Who asks something like that after a kiss?" I couldn't meet his eyes for some reason.

"Baby, this is all very new to me. Please tell me if anything is wrong".

"Dean, stop. Nothing is wrong. You are a good kisser. Now let's watch some sunset that is supposed to be so beautiful".

"Sure, boss. What will you do if I tell you that I suddenly don't want to watch the frigging sunset and I have found some better way to kill the time?"

I blushed harder, if it was even possible. "Will you stop it? Don't distract me. I don't want to miss the sunset"

"It's sunset, baby, not a shooting star. Anyway, I am glad I have that effect on you"

I punched his arms and wished that my flustered state was not so obvious. He smiled and held my hands.

The silence was comfortable and the sunset was as beautiful as he promised. But it was only the second highlight of the evening after that kiss.

Chapter 27

I realized I was just passing through life until I met Dean. It seems like an over used line, but he did change my view on my daily routine. Everything seemed better with him.

My morning coffee seemed to give me more energy when I had it with him and my day was more interesting when I shared it with him.

I have gone camping and watched the stars hundreds of times but nothing compared to today. He told me that he was planning for us to set up a tent there but he couldn't get the permission on time. So we settled for a picnic and having our dinner there.

He made sandwiches for us to eat picnic-style. Basket and all. When I asked about it, he said he wanted to do it right. "When I thought of ideas for a picnic, I remembered seeing this in many movies and series. Is this ok?"

"I hope you are talking about rom-coms and not true crime like the ones I watch".

"Haha, so funny. I enjoy true crime too but I get my references from cheesy old movies".

I shook my head and took a bite of the sandwich. It was delicious. "It's really good. You didn't tell me that you are a good cook".

"It is one of the things I can make well. I couldn't make any complicated dishes like you", he confessed.

"Don't worry. I will take care of the cooking part. You can focus on being my taste-tester". I loved cooking for him, anyway.

"You would cook for me daily? You also want me around always like I do?"

"Yes, it might be shocking but I actually enjoy your company. You make my days better". It was the first time I said it out loud to him. It was liberating to say what's on my mind without filters.

"You made my day, you know? I thought I was the only one who had these kind of thoughts and you might get tired of me being clingy".

"Dean, don't ever think that. I am glad you can't read minds because I have no idea what you would do if you know what's going on there".

"That sounds dirty, baby. Did you mean it that way? Do you have some secret fantasy to see me dressed up in a certain way or to tie me up? I am ok either way".

Oh my God! He didn't actually say that did he? We were losing our filters and I loved it even if it drove me crazy.

"You are crazy", I deadpanned. I couldn't meet his eyes or I might start something we can't finish in this place.

He held my face and turned me to face him. "Baby, I was just teasing. But I need to stop if I don't want to start something we can't finish here and now".

Can he actually read minds? I loved how our wavelengths matched even on some crazy dirty levels.

"Um, yeah, we don't want that, do we?" I coughed to cover up my embarrassment.

"Do you want to come over to my place? I haven't taken you there yet, right?".

I nodded not trusting my voice. Did I want to go? Sure. Did I trust myself? No. But was I ready? Heck yeah.

The drive back was electric as I felt some tension in the air and I didn't know what to do. He seemed the same way. Eventually he put on some music and started singing along which eased some nervousness, at least on my side.

"We are here", he announced. I took in the house in front of me. It was a two storey building and he told me that he was staying on the second floor. He was sharing the house with two of his friends.

We took the elevator and went up to his room. He stopped as the door was unlocked and he visibly tensed up a little.

I touched his shoulder. "Are you ok? Did you forget to lock the door?"

"No, looks like my father decided to visit. Sorry I didn't know he was coming over. Are you ok with meeting him today?"

"Sure, I wanted to meet him anyway. Are you cool with me meeting him today?"

"It was not the activity I had in my mind but this could be good too", he winked and we were back to normal now. "Come on, now I can't wait for you to meet him finally".

We entered the house and he called "Father, are you in the kitchen? I brought someone for you to meet".

"Yeah, I am in here, why there are expired food in the fridge? Are you not eating well, Dean? Wait, did you bring someone? Do you mean Alex?"

I was not prepared to meet his father but nothing in the world could have prepared me for what I saw.

Chapter 28

- -

I saw a guy in his mid or late thirties coming out of the kitchen wearing an apron that said "Fcuk cooking!".

"Hello, sir. Um, I am Alex" I couldn't help but stare at him in disbelief. I expected someone old and wise looking. I didn't know why I expected someone like that but hey, Dean calls him father and told me he was an actual angel. Can you blame me?

"Hi Alex, I have heard a lot about you, I mean a lot. Nice to finally meet you". He extended his hands for me to shake but then changed his mind and pulled me in for a hug.

I was surprised and not at all mildly. I thought he would be all business-like and strict. I imagined he would actually yell at me or something for making Dean to spill the secret but not this.

"I am Keith Rogane. Sorry I couldn't give you my actual name. Protocols, you know? Feel free to call me whatever you want though. Father or Key or Roge. Anything is fine". Dean was stifling his laugh on seeing my shocked face.

What? How am I supposed to call him "Key"?

"Thank you, Mr.Rogane. I have heard a lot about you too".

"Mr.Rogane? I think he is still in shock", He told Dean. "Alex, don't be too formal. Call me Keith. Make yourself at home. I make killer enchiladas. Do you want some?".

"Uh, may be next time, Sir, I mean Keith. We just had dinner".

"Speak for yourself, Alex. I can not pass up on father's enchiladas. Those are really amazing. Father, Alex doesn't know what he is missing. Give him some too". Dean insisted that I have some and may God bless him.

Those were heavenly. Pun intended. The initial nervousness I had seemed useless now.

We were watching reality shows which Dean liked. I could see where he was getting all the yelling from. Keith made me feel welcome throughout the night and I didn't feel the time passing by. It was around midnight and suddenly I remembered I had a house to return and a wardrobe to fold.

"Sorry to interrupt, but I need to go back now. I didn't notice the time and it's already midnight. Thanks for the enchiladas, I would love to have them again".

"Is that you way of saying you would like to meet me again? Dean wasn't joking. I like the way you speak. You can stay here if you like. I am leaving soon and wouldn't be in your way".

"What? No, no. I planned on leaving soon, anyway. I left my dishes in the sink. And let's not forget about the clothes I have to fold. So, um, yeah, I need to go back. You are not in our way. You can stay as long you want".

Both of them seemed amused at my outburst. "Calm down, Alex. You can go home if you want. Dean, drop him safely. I would like to spend time with you again, son. Thanks for making Dean happy".

"I need to say thank you for taking care of Dean. And for making me feel welcome. Take care, Key".

"Hey! You took my suggestion, finally. See you around, kid". He gave me a hug and we left.

"So, that was your father. A heads-up would have been nice" I said as Dean started the car.

"Hey, I didn't plan for the meeting to happen so soon. I didn't think that you would be shocked. But normal dads are old and different, I guess. As he is an angel, he doesn't age, I thought you would have figured".

"Ahh, I didn't think of that. He could pass as your brother if you haven't told me. I like his sense of humor too. You are lucky to have him"

"Should I be jealous of my father, now? Jokes apart, yes I am really lucky to have him as my family"

I shook my head at him and wondered how I found this adorable guy. Wait, he found me. I just had to thank my lucky stars for that almost-accident. Sounds like a horrible thing to be grateful for, but look where it got me.

I smiled at my own thoughts. "Care to share, baby?" Dean interrupted my blissful thoughts.

"Nothing, I was just thanking my stars for the almost-accident which led me to meet you".

"Even if there was no accident, I would have tried to speak to you then. I couldn't stay away anymore".

Welcome back, butterflies. They have got the license to come and go back as they please.

"Really? I might not have talked to a stranger. I watch too many true crime documentaries for my own good".

"Wanna bet? I have seen the look you gave me on the first day. I could sense that you were interested. That's why I had the courage to go after you". Did I tell you he was arrogant in an adorable way?

"God! Was I that obvious?" I closed my eyes in disbelief and prayed that I would become invisible.

"Baby, don't be shy. What's wrong in being interested on someone? I told you I liked you from the beginning. You need not hide from me"

"I love it when you have no filters. Can I ask you something?" He nodded so I went ahead and asked him. "Why did you wait to talk to me again till we met by chance near the gas station?"

"Uh, I thought you were interested but I didn't feel as confident as now back then. I didn't want to put you at risk too, because I didn't know how father would react. But after meeting you at the gas station I couldn't stop myself"

"I am glad you talked to me. I can't say for sure if I would have acted on my crush"

"Aww, was it just a crush? I thought you were obsessed", He teased.

"Sounds like you are describing yourself". For once I had a better comeback. Yes, the universe is finally on my side.

"You got that right, baby". I came to a conclusion that I was transported to the world of cheesy rom-coms and I loved every moment of it.

Chapter 29

The next week I was still getting used to have a boyfriend around. We texted most of the times. He drove me to and from the work. And I made breakfast and dinner for him daily. We watched true crime and reality shows alternatively.

On Friday morning he seemed to be on a good mood. He was whistling when I made breakfast.

"Are you ok? I know it's Friday and weekend is almost here, so we can be cheerful. But you seem a little extra happy today. What's the occasion?"

"I was waiting for you to ask. You remember? I wanted to take you camping for our first date but I didn't get the permit at the last minute".

I nodded my head and asked him to continue.

"I found a campsite a little further away from the city and want to take you there this weekend. You want to go?"

"Heck yeah! I love camping. I have always went alone but I want to go with you now"

"Pack your bags today baby, we can leave tomorrow morning. After your saturday sleep-in of course"

I just smiled and kissed him to show my appreciation. We sneaked in few kisses here and there but didn't have time to have a full-on make out session until now.

His kisses were soft and sweet at first but when I opened my mouth it became frantic. He used his tongue to explore my mouth and I forgot my name there.

I had to leave for office in few minutes and I had half the mind to call in sick today. No one would mind, right? But Dean said he had to take care of an important business today.

I thought of asking Dean to check the time but immediately abandoned that thought as his lips moved to my neck. Now I forgot the place I lived. Were we even on Earth? My mind floated on zero gravity.

Dean was kissing my neck with a force that would actually leave a hickey. Bye bye, my V-neck sweater. I might have to wear some collar shirt. Speaking of shirt, when did my hand go inside of his shirt?

I didn't notice that, but well, I wouldn't remove it even if I was held at gun point. When I touched his abs he took a sharp breath and stopped his heavenly work on my neck and looked into my eyes.

Suddenly I was so aware of my hands and felt so shy to remove them and so awkward to keep them there.

"Uhh, I didn't know you went to the gym". Sue me, I couldn't think of anything clever now.

He burst out laughing and I removed my hands from under his shirt, clearly embarrassed.

"Baby, I am sorry. But you always crack me up. I didn't expect for you to say anything like that".

I was laughing a little myself relieved that he enjoyed my quirki-ness, which is a translation for filter-less mouth.

"And to answer your question, yes, I go to gym whenever I get time. I want to take care of my health. You can come with me if you want".

"Sure, sure" I was still flustered.

He looked embarassed now. "About that, I didn't know what I was thinking. I wanted to kiss you and hold you tighter. I have, um, never done that with anyone. Please tell me if you are not comfortable with anything".

"What? Oh, m-me too. I would not feel uncomfortable with you. I was also not thinking, certainly not about your abs. I mean stomach. No, I mean your body. Ugh, it sounds creepy, doesn't it?"

"No, baby. As I have already said, you need not be shy to show your desire, not with me. Sorry to leave a mark, though". He touched my neck lightly and I shivered at the memory of his lips on the same spot.

"You don't look sorry" I playfully swatted his hands.

"Right, I am somewhat proud of my work. So that people would know you are taken"

"Ooh, didn't take you for the type to mark your territory", I teased.

"Just kidding, baby. Do you want to change your shirt? I can help you with that". He threw in a wink.

"Jerk. Wait here. I will change my shirt. We are already late and I don't want to miss half day of work" I sighed dramatically.

He laughed and I went in to change my shirt. I admired his work in the mirror and hoped my collar shirt would cover that because I could just imagine Rose's scream.

The scream was louder than the one I imagined. Because it came from Rose who was joined by George. Safe to say my shirt collar didn't do a very good job in covering up the evidence.

"Spill the beans, now", Rose used the voice which meant business. So I spilled, after some cuts, of course. I couldn't tell her or anyone about the angel thing.

Rose sighed dreamily. "Your wait was worth it. You found the one, finally".

George was nodding his head. "So glad you found someone, man. Congratulations"

"Thanks. I would like to introduce you guys. But we are going camping this weekend, so I will ask him when he will be free next week".

"Ooh, camping. Sounds naughty! Finish that hickey business, will ya?" Rose wouldn't give up opportunities to tease me. I blushed on cue. "Stop it, Rose. It is not a hickey, just a mosquito bite" I tried to lie my way out of it.

"Yeah, I have seen the mosquito bites, trust me. Looks like this big mosquito is named Dean. On a serious note, I can't wait to go on double dates".

"I would not want to interfere on your dates" It was my turn to tease.

"Oh shut up! You know what I mean". Rose was quick to respond.

"Haha ok Rose. I will ask Dean". I would be genuinely happy if we can all hang out.

Chapter 30

I was packing with all the enthusiasm in the world when Dean called me.

"Baby, did you see the news? There is a storm coming so we couldn't go camping this weekend. I am so sorry".

I was deeply disappointed. Before I could fake some chirpiness and say that we could go next time, Dean spoke again. "I have already packed my bags and told my father that I would be away for the weekend. Shall I come to your house? We can have a movie marathon. Or something. Your pick".

"Yes, yes. That sounds fun. Can't wait. When are you coming?"

"How about right away?"

"That works. Pick up a carton of eggs and milk on your way".

"Way ahead of you, baby. Already bought the groceries and packed 'em. Do you need anything else?"

"No, drive safely, Dean".

"See you soon, baby". I was suddenly hyper aware of the situation. Dean. In my house. For the weekend.

Did I clean the house recently? Did I leave my underwear any-where? Is the bed comfortable enough for him?

My head was spiraling imagining all the possible scenarios. I needed expert opinion so I called Rose.

"Wassup, Lexy? You want to know which underwear to pack for your camping trip? How about nothing?"

"Geez, Rose. It's really a camping trip and it won't be probably like anything from your imagination. Anyway, camping is no-go because of the storm. Dean is staying with me for the weekend"

"Wow. This is even better. It would be better if it's the environment is familiar to you".

"Better for what?"

"God! Do I need to spell it for you, Alex? It will be your first time with him, right?"

"Um, that, yeah. We fooled around a bit but things might happen this weekend, I guess"

"I was right. There are no mosquitoes. Go Dean!"

"I am freaking out here, a little help for your bestie?"

"It might sound like a usual advise but go with the flow, Lexy. Don't think too much. I know you would. You trust him, right?"

"Yeah" I whispered.

"Make right choices. And hey, don't forget to text me the details. Even if it is R-rated. Especially R-rated".

"Gross. Forget this call ever happened. Bye, Rose". I hung up the call. Typical Rose. But still she was right. I should not over-think and ruin this.

"Baby, you in there? Come and get this grocery bag". Dean's voice interrupted my thoughts.

I went to get the bag and stopped few seconds to admire him. He was in his usual jeans and t-shirt attire but still managed to take my breath away.

"Baby, we have all weekend to drool over each other. Now take this bag". He gave me his infamous wink.

"Get over yourself. I was just checking if you brought everything", I tried to brush him off.

But he knows me better. He came inside and trapped me between his arms. "Yeah, right. You were looking like you were ready to eat. Sure, but not the food".

As usual my brain decided it was time to take a break. "Um, uh, yeah, I am hungry. I mean I could eat. I mean dinner". For each word his face came closer to mine and I totally forgot what I was blabbering about. Dinner, what?

"But I am really starving, though. Let's get something to eat first". He gave a quick peck and moved away, much to my disappointment. I pouted and followed him.

We had dinner. I had frozen pizza in the fridge and special occasion calls for trusty old pizza.

"Do you want to take a shower first?" I asked him without thinking.

He looked at me with a little shock in his eyes and then I realized what that implied.

"I mean, there is only one bathroom. So I wanted to check if you wanted to go first or if I could"

"Oh, ahem, you can go ahead. I want to put away some groceries and do a little unpacking". I nodded and practically ran to the bathroom while he was laughing at my expense.

I have showered and put on my comfy pants and t-shirt. And checked my reflection in the mirror. That's something new. I liked the version staring back at me. He looked happy and carefree.

"Baby, shall I use your shampoo? I forgot mine". I heard Dean asking from the bathroom.

"Yeah, it's fine", I replied.

"Do you want to come and find it for me?"

He never stops, does he? "Nah, you can come out with stinky hair for all I care".

"You love my hair and you know it"

"Sure, whatever helps you sleep at night"

"Oh, baby. Wouldn't you want to know?"

"I finished dressing. I will be watching TV in the hall if you ever come out of that bathroom", I said and I bolted. I couldn't survive longer there.

Finally he finished showering and decided to grace me with his presence. He had wet hair and drying it which was not a sight I was used to. My heart did somersaults and I couldn't stop looking at him.

"Don't bite your lips when you are looking at me, Alex. It makes me want to do things to you"

"Where did you learn to speak like that? Must be the daytime soap operas" I was seriously wondering.

"I am serious. It's like I have no filter around you and my mouth has a brain of it's own"

He sounds just like me. I often think the same thing. "Do you want my help in drying your hair?"

"Do you even need to ask?"

I took the towel from him and started drying his hair. Let me tell you, there is something intimate in doing that. He grabbed my hands and pulled me down to his lap.

"This is like torture. I can't take it, baby"

"Oh, sorry. Was I being harsh? I thought I did it gently"

"What? No, I wasn't talking about that. My hair is fine. You make me crazy, you know that, right?"

I shook my head. He cupped my cheeks. "You are adorable". Kiss. "You are sweet". Kiss. "You look hot". Kiss. "Did I miss anything?"

"I love you", I decided it was the best time to say it.

"Wait. Really? I have been waiting to say it from our first date, you know? I didn't want to freak you out. But you went ahead and told me. This is what drives me crazy. You are so amazing. I know I am rambling but I love you too. A lot".

"Thanks, Dean, for everything", I said with sincerity.

"Baby, I should be the one to thank you. You changed my life. Even if you didn't know, you did that just by existing"

"I don't know what to say. I am not good with words"

"I know some other way". He kissed me in a sweet way. Then he held out his hand. I took it and intertwined our fingers.

Chapter 31

"What do you want to do?" Dean asked me.

"I don't know. We usually watch true crime shows or the variety shows that you like"

"Sure but let's make it a game". Dean said with twinkling eyes.

"What do you have in that devil mind of yours?" I was thrilled at his smirk.

"Here is the rule. Let's watch "crime files" first. But we need to predict the culprit. If I win, you take off an item of your clothing and if you win, I will do it"

I was really amazed and a little skeptical. "Come on, where did you get the idea from?"

"Ever heard of strip poker? I thought we could customize it for our tastes. We can watch variety shows next and predict the winner. Same penalty though"

"Sounds interesting" was all I could manage. My heart was going a hundred miles per second.

"Baby, sorry if I put you in an uncomfortable position. I thought it would be fun. Forget it. Let's just watch the shows"

"What? No, I never back out of a dare. Let's do the strip show. That sounds wrong. Let's think about a name later"

He was laughing already. "Ok, let's see what you got. Pun unintended. Or was it?"

I slapped his arms and switched on the TV to load the latest episodes of my favorite true crime series. Come on culprit, show yourself.

We decided to write down the culprit at the same time at the half way mark to avoid cheating.

First episode was easy for me. It was the husband and I got it right. If you watch a lot of true crime shows, you would know.

He took off his shirt even though he was wearing socks. When I asked him about it, he said he needed socks to keep him warm. Yeah, right. Show off.

I guessed the second one wrong. And I proceeded to take off my socks but he protested. "Eye for an eye, shirt for a shirt" he said. So I took off my t-shirt and I was suddenly feeling hot. Weird. I expected it would be cold.

Will I be called a psycho if I wished that the truck driver stole the family heirlooms? I thought you were helping, distant cousin. Ugh, killers were my strong forte, not thieves. We moved on to his favorite spin-the-wheel show.

I tried to concentrate on the spinning wheel in the show to predict the winner but I was distracted by the shirtless Dean flexing in front of me whenever he gets a chance.

Needless to say, I lost the next one and took off my socks much to his protest.

The next game had twists and we both failed to guess the winner. "What now?" I asked Dean.

"I haven't expected this situation. We both take off an item of clothing? Sounds fair, right?"

"Or we both keep it on?" I tried to convince him.

"Hey, the rules state that if we fail to guess, we have to take it off. I didn't make it up"

"You did though".

"So, shall I take off two clothing items? I can take the hit for you", he offered.

"No, game is a game. I will do it". I took off my pants and was left with my underwear. He still had on his pants. Not fair.

It was his turn to get distracted. He kept staring at my legs and ended up predicting the winner wrong. He was more than happy to take off his pants which defeated the purpose of my celebrations.

So, we settled for one last episode to see who was winning our stripping game. We both felt distracted by the lack of clothes and the air seemed charged and different. I could hear the tiniest bit of sounds and we could not look each other in the eyes.

I suddenly felt thirsty and reached out for the water in the table. He did the same and our fingers brushed. He turned to look at me and I did the same.

I don't remember if he kissed me first or I did. Or if we met half way. We started kissing like there was no tomorrow.

He pulled me to his lap and I was straddling him. But we never broke off the kiss. I never knew I had it in me to kiss someone so passionately.

He lifted me up and carried to the bedroom. He set me down gently on the mattress.

"Do you want to continue? If you are not ready, we can wait Alex".

"Ooh, sounds serious. I am a big boy and I can tell you if I am not comfortable, Dean. Now shut up and kiss me".

That was all the confirmation he needed. "God! That was hot". With that he started to kiss me with even more passion if that was possible.

As the clothes business was already taken care of, we had all the time in the world to kiss each other and explore each other's bodies.

I am not going to lie. I have had fantasies of making love during a thunderstorm, but the reality was much hotter than any fantasies. Or may be I was not that creative.

The next morning I woke up with an amazing feeling I couldn't describe in words.

I opened my eyes and expected to see Dean sleeping peacefully but he was awake and staring at me with a smile. He was extra hot with the bedhead look.

"That's supposed to be creepy but you pull that off too. That isn't fair" I pouted.

"You called me creepy and disguised it in a compliment? I am impressed, love".

"Love? Why do you sound like a British protagonist in a badly directed series?"

"I wanted to try some other nicknames. Does sunshine work for you?"

"You can call me by any name you want. I love it when you call me baby. I am fine with anything" I replied honestly.

"But I want you to call out my name like you did last night". He touched my cheeks and smirked playfully.

The conversation took a 360 degree turn from sweet to hot. "When you do things you did last night, I will call your name like

I did last night". That's right. I woke up and chose to be sassy. Deal with it.

"When I thought you couldn't get any more hotter. You keep proving me wrong, love".

"That will be my lifetime job. Now get up and make me some coffee".

"Yes, boss. Do you want some breakfast too?"

"I was kidding. You can stay in bed if you want. I will make breakfast as usual".

"No, I am serious, baby. I will take care of you today. And tomorrow. And day after tomorrow. Screw it. All the upcoming tomorrows. What do you think?"

"Stop being cheesy, angel. Let me take care of the breakfast. Go and fix your stinky breath".

"You weren't complaining last night. Is it bad? Can you check again?" He showered me with little kisses and I melted.

"Ok, I was kidding. Now stop before this turns into someth-". Well, he did stop. He stopped me with his knee-weakening kiss.

It's safe to say we decided to have brunch as the breakfast time was well over when we decided to leave the bed. No one told me skipping breakfast would be this fun.

Chapter 32

Y ou know it won't be always rainbows and sunshine when you start to date somebody.

I believed we were the exception. Rookie mistake. Let me start from the beginning.

It was going very well with me cooking breakfast and dinner and us taking turns to stay at each other's houses.

We had fallen into a perfect routine. He came up with creative nickname for me everyday and I struggled with coming up with anything other than the obvious 'angel'. He didn't seem to mind.

But lately Dean have been busy with some works the details of which he didn't want to bore me with. His words, not mine.

As I got used to the attention, I craved it when I got it so little. I was alone before I met him but that guy ruined me with all his nicknames.

Still, I decided to give him some space and didn't want to sound like a clingy boyfriend desperate for attention even when I was one.

So that day, I was leaving town for a week for a seminar and I asked Dean to drive me to the airport in the morning.

He said he had a small work but he still came and dropped me at the airport. When I was away, he barely texted me. He didn't call at all.

I complained to Rose but she asked me if I trusted Dean and the answer was "always". So she asked me specifically not to over-think and complicate the situation.

You know what is my kryptonite? Doing exactly what I am told not to do.

So I went ahead and created all these possible scenarios in my head and became anxious to return home.

Once I reached home, I called Dean and asked him to come to my house. He came and he looked a lot tired and disheveled and not in a sexy way.

In all the time we dated, I have never seen him like that and I started to panic. Was he dying? I don't think so. He had angel grace, right?

"Are you ok, Dean? You look, uh, tired".

"Baby, sit down. I want to tell you something".

I started freaking out. "What is it? Are you dying? Are we breaking up? Did you meet someone else?"

"Alex, calm down. I am not dying. It's nothing like that. Listen to me. I am not leaving you. Not now. Not ever. Do you understand?"

I nodded, feeling a bit ashamed of my outburst.

"That day, when I drove you to the airport, I had to make sure someone was safe, you know, as a part of my job". I nodded again, encouraging him to continue. He held my hands.

"But I left them for some time to drive you to the airport. I asked my friend to take over for sometime but he had another emergency and I didn't pick his call because I was driving. That person had a minor accident and my father was not happy. So I couldn't talk to you properly. At least not over the text. I'm sorry, baby".

I was not prepared for this. "Oh God! I am really sorry. I shouldn't have asked you to drive me. I behaved like a clingy boyfriend when you had some important work".

"What? No, baby. Don't blame yourself. You have every right to act however you want. I should have been more careful. Don't worry. It was nothing serious and father understands me".

"What if it was serious? Did you get punished? Did your father scold you?"

"No, baby. He was a bit disappointed. But these things happen. We can not protect everyone 24/7. Right? Anyway, I told my father that I was quitting".

"You told what? Dean, don't tell me it was because of me".

"I want to spend time with you, baby. And take care of you properly. Don't worry. Father is ok with my decision".

Then I let my stupid over-thinking brain take over.

"Stop, Dean. You are making a mistake and I wouldn't allow it. I know how much important your job is to you. I can not let you give up on your dream. How long have you known me? 6 months? Your dream have been with you longer than that. I don't want to stand in your way. Let's break up. It's easy to do it now rather than later regretting it".

"What? Baby, calm down. You don't mean that, do you?"

"Yes, Dean. God! Stop treating me like I am a kid. I can make decisions and I don't want to be with you anymore. Do you understand?"

When I saw his face, I wanted to apologize and kiss him to make it all feel better. But I couldn't. I shouldn't. He might be able to give up his job now but he will later regret it. That's how life works.

"Baby, hear me out. Please don't do this".

"No, Dean. I am serious. Please leave, now". I was afraid if I let him stay few more seconds, my resolve would crumble.

He stood up and left without any words. He was such a gentleman at the very end too. He was right. I was the baby as I was always acting like one.

Chapter 33

It was safe to say I didn't go to office that day. Rose called me and came over to my house immediately after she heard my voice on the phone.

"God! Alex! What happened to you? Did you eat walnut cake? I know it is delicious but you are allergic". Her attempt made me smile despite my situation.

"I broke up with Dean" I told her in between sniffles.

"Oh God! Why? Did he break your heart? Where is he? Let me give him a piece of my mind".

"He didn't. I did. He quit his important job for me. I didn't want him to. He will regret it in the future. He might regret us. So I broke it off early. I can barely survive now. I can't imagine how it will be after few years. I don't know what to do Rose".

She smacked me in the back of my head. I looked at her in confusion. Did she hear my sad story?

"You are an idiot, Alex. Did you let your over-thinking brain take over? You know he is a little bitch".

"I know, but I can't help it". My tears started flowing again.

"Don't cry, Alex. What did he say? He just up and left when you told him? He didn't fight?"

"I was too harsh on him. Oh God! He had a rough time and I didn't even try to make him better. I was so selfish. Who would want me? No wonder he left".

"Alex, stop. You did what you felt right at that moment. We all make mistakes. The concept of apologizing exists for all of us. Go to him and explain. He will understand".

"But, Rose, I don't want to stand in between his dreams. His job is important to him. To his father. I don't want him to hate me for this later".

"So you have decided to make it better by breaking his heart now?"

"When you put it that way it sounds really selfish of me. Whose side are you on?"

"Your side, Alex. You were so happy with him. Happiest since I have known you. So I am trying to talk some sense to you. But I know you wouldn't change your decision. You have to sit and think about it. Do you promise to reconsider?"

I just nodded. As she had some urgent work at the office, she had to leave.

I was alone with my thoughts. Not a good company at that moment.

I realized I didn't give him a chance to explain. I was too harsh. But then I was right about him regretting the decision later.

I don't know how much time I spent thinking all of these and when I fell asleep on the sofa. I woke up when my phone rang and disappointed a bit that Rose was calling and not Dean.

"Hi Rose" I answered the phone and heard a car stopping in front of my house.

"Lexy, come out. Let's go for a drive. It's urgent. Please come".

There was an urgency in her voice and I was genuinely concerned. "Are you ok? I'm c-"

The line got disconnected. I shook my head and opened the door for her.

"Can you change into something more presentable, please?" Rose raised her eyebrows at my choice of wardrobe.

"Why? Where are we going? You sounded a bit off. Are you ok?"

"I will tell you later, Lexy. You trust your best friend, right? Then change into something good and come meet me in the car in 5 minutes. Go! Go! Go!" So I went.

I put on some nice clothes I could find and got into her car. She started driving and after sometime I realized where she was taking me.

"Rose, why are we going there? I am not ready to face him yet. Can you please turn around?"

"Alex, please hear him out for a minute. That's all I ask. For me. Please. If not, you will be the one with regrets".

"Fine", I sulked, living upto my nickname.

She stopped in front of Dean's condo and asked me to get down.

I saw the banner on the front saying "Congratulations, Dean" and I was really confused. Did people celebrate break up?

"Rose, what's going on?" I realized that she drove away. I was going to kill her.

I stood there with confusion when I heard his voice. "Baby! You came!". It took everything in me to not to run into his arms.

"Uh, Rose drove me and left me here. What's going on? Is this a break up party?"

"What? Who broke up? Oh, God, No. We are not broken up. I won't let you go without a fight".

"Dean, you know I am stubborn and you couldn't change my mind that easily".

"I know better than anyone, Alex. Give me 15 minutes to change your mind. Am I not worth at least 15 minutes of your day?"

He was worth more than that. I would give him my lifetime if he asks but he doesn't need to know that.

"Ok, 15 minutes. That's it".

He visibly relaxed. "Come on, baby. We have a party to attend".

We went upstairs and people cheered when they saw Dean.

He politely excused himself and pulled me to his bedroom.

"Hey, I didn't agree to 15 minutes of this. I thought you wanted to explain".

He laughed. I was falling again for him when I heard that sound. Snap out of it, Alex.

"Baby, I love you for your dirty mind. But we are not here for it. At least not now. I just wanted some privacy".

"Yeah, that's what I meant too. Talk. You have 10 minutes left. You wasted 5 by laughing at my expense".

Chapter 34

I was waiting for the explanation. He took a deep breath and took my hands in his.

"Here's the deal. I would have quit my job even if I didn't meet you. I told my father I would be quitting soon as I wanted a normal life and my father was more than happy for me to have one. I was taking classes at the university and I almost completed my research paper when I met you". Wow! I didn't have a clue.

"I took a break for a while and for the past month I have been working on my graduation on the side. I wanted it to be a surprise so I didn't say anything to you. I am sorry that I made you feel lonely. It was never my intention but it's not an excuse. My father was disappointed because I hid it from you and overworked myself. It was not your fault at all".

I was shocked. I couldn't believe I lost almost a day with him because I was stubborn and jumped to conclusions.

"Oh my God! I don't even know what I can say to apologize to you. I didn't even talk with you before taking a decision all by myself and ruined graduation day for you. I thought I knew what was the best for you".

"Baby, stop it. I should have told you. But let's stop the blame game. We already lost almost a day because of this. I don't want to waste even a second more".

Then I attacked him. Yes, that's the proper way to describe it. Only I did it with my lips to which he enthusiastically reciprocated.

"Congratulations, Dean. Sorry I didn't get you any present"

"It's ok baby, I might ask for something later". There it was. His wink, which could heal my heart.

"Seriously, you are the one with the dirtiest mind no matter how bad the situation is!"

"What? I thought we reconciled. Haven't you learned anything? The protagonists make up by frantically kissing each other".

It was my turn to laugh. "Imaginary protagonists, Dean. No one does that in re-". I was effectively silenced by his lips on mine.

"Was it frantic enough?" He asked between kisses.

"Your friends are waiting outside. Let's go, Dean".

"Then why are you clutching my shirt tightly?" He smirked.

"It was for, well, balance. Let's go before they start wondering".

"What is there to wonder? Two people who are dating goes into bedroom for few minutes. People know what's going on".

"What? Oh my God! You are right. Let's go out, now".

"Sure, baby. Let's continue later when there is no disturbance". I slapped his arms.

"Get you mind out of the gutter". But he doesn't have to know that I was in there with him.

We went out and made small talk with his friends. Rose came in with Jake and George and finally I made the boyfriend introduction that was long due.

They all hit it off and were soon laughing at my expense. Great! Just what I wanted. Still I loved every moment with him. I mean, look at that amazing goofball, who wouldn't love him?

Finally, everyone went home, leaving us alone. Not that I was waiting for this time. Ok, you got me. I was waiting but not for what you have in mind. But to ask him few questions.

"Dean, shall I ask you something?"

"Baby, you can ask me anything".

"So, you quit. What now? Does your father take back his grace? And he gives it to someone else? Do you look for a job now? You are not going out of town, are you?"

"I am not going anywhere. I will stay by your side even if you try to push me away. Don't worry, baby. I got a job to teach at the school which comes under my father's organization. It's my dream to help others. I don't care about the way I do it. And the grace part is correct. It's something like that except I gave it back to my father already. Um, before I came to see you today. I was going to tell you but you wouldn't hear it".

"Right, sorry about that. Won't happen again, I promise".

"No more apologies. Let's move on. This is supposed to be a new journey for me. And I am lucky to start it with you".

I hugged him tightly to show my support and love for him. He hugged me back and patted my back.

"I promise to never let you go again, Dean. I love you".

"That's what I needed to hear, baby. I love you too. More than you realize. Now, where were we before you worried about people interrupting us?"

"I believe you were supposed to collect your graduation present from me".

"And make up for the lost time".

"Yeah, that too. Are you ready, angel?"

"I am not an angel anymore, baby. You have to come up with some other nickname".

"You will always be my angel. You promised, remember?"

"Yes baby. I am your angel and I am always at your service".

"Then, what are you waiting for?" These words were enough for him to close the distance between us. He lifted me up and carried me to the bedroom where we picked up exactly where we left before.

Epilogue

It was a routine day from the life of an angel (not literally) and his baby.

"Dean, breakfast is ready. Have something before you leave".

"Coming, baby". He came into the kitchen looking sharp. You will be irritated if I use any more adjectives to describe his good looks, won't you?

But I won't let that stop me. He was wearing a blue button down shirt which I chose for him and his khaki work pants. Let's say I would ask him to come home early for some private lessons. I know my mind is dirty and I am not going to apologize for it.

He pecked my cheek oblivious to my dirty thoughts. Who was I kidding? He might be having a few of his own right now.

"I love that apron on you, baby. Can you wear it tonight? Only the apron though". See, I have told you.

"Dean, you are a teacher now. Behave yourself".

"I am a teacher once I enter the school. But at home I am your boyfriend. I have taken that role seriously".

"Right, what do you want for dinner today?"

"You". His one word can set free millions of butterflies in my stomach. He still has that effect on me. Even after all these months. I punched him lightly on his stomach and he held my hands.

"Baby, it's always up to you. I will be happy to eat whatever you cook".

"Ok. I will make something new today. I can't wait for you to try it, love".

"Aww, I can't get enough of you calling me 'love'. I want to hear it again tonight". He winked at me.

"Don't push it, Dean". I was fake scowling and he knew it.

He left after few kisses and I decided to work from home today. After finishing my works, I made enchiladas for dinner. And yes, I got the recipe from Keith, Dean's father.

It turned out good but not much as Keith's but I can live with that.

Dean came back in the evening. "What's smelling so good? Apart from you, I mean".

He still got his flirting game. I had to give him that. "I made your father's famous enchiladas. I figured you might miss him".

"A bit. I see him less often than before. But it's fine. Both of us are busy. Anyway, you are the best, baby".

"Wash up and come have dinner with me".

"These are really good". Dean liked the food and I was glad. One little word and smile from him makes all my efforts worth it. I know I sound like a sappy guy from bad rom-com. But see if I care.

"Baby, I have been meaning to ask you. Shall I move in with you? I am a teacher now and I don't think it is economically wise to have an extra house that I barely visit".

"Oh my God! Sure, Dean. Are you having trouble with money? I can't believe I accepted that watch from you as a birthday gift. Shall we return it and get the money back?"

"Shh, baby. I am sorry. I am not having any money problems. My father is paying me well. I have some savings too. I thought it would be too soon to ask to move in together. You might think I am weird. So I tried something else. I didn't mean to make you feel worried".

"Dean, I am going to kill you. I have told you to speak your mind always. What do you mean by 'I might think you are weird'? I already know that. I love you, weirdness and all. So let's move in together".

"I love you the most, baby. I don't know what to say! Let me show you instead. Why don't you go and get that apron?"

With that he kissed me and then let's just say that my wish for some private lessons came true that night.